Melody Harper, Submissive of Darkness

A Werewolf and Vampire Spanking Romance

Melody Harper, Submissive of Darkness

A Werewolf and Vampire Spanking Romance

Clarine Klein

ISBN: 978-1-7339350-9-8
Imprint: Studio Bebop Inc.

Cover Illustration by Arkham-Insanity
https://www.patreon.com/isadoraarkham
https://twitter.com/ArkhamInsanity

What happens when a bratty vampire bites off more than she can chew?

College freshman and recently-turned vampire, Melody Harper, is trying to live her best unlife. Fresh out of the closet and eager to make up for lost time, she goes hunting for a date / midnight snack at the local girl bar just off campus. Only problem is, the muscular butch she's set her sights on turns out to be a werewolf Alpha who doesn't take too kindly to involuntary blood donations.

Morgan Bloodfang can't believe her luck when the most adorable baby goth she's ever seen starts flirting with her while she's out drinking one night. Plump in all the right places and with a submissive streak a mile wide, she's just her type. Only problem is, her shy dance partner turns out to have eyes bigger than her stomach when she passes out on top of her after going for her jugular.

Escorting the unconscious girl home, Morgan fully intends on giving her a piece of her mind (and a dose of her belt) once she wakes up, only to end up claiming her as her mate instead. It might be sudden, but instinct has never led her astray before, and she doubts it will now. Only problem is, Melody is a gigantic brat, and if they're going to make things work, she's going to have to learn her place.

Over her Alpha's knee.

CHAPTER 1

Melody

Gritting my teeth to keep myself from chickening out (again), I stepped from between the shadows of two motorcycles near the back of the parking lot outside the Jackalope.

"All right, Melody, no backing down. You can do this, you hot, sexy, um… hottie."

Pushing through the wall of lingering secondhand smoke that hung over everything like a shroud, I smoothed down the front of my top for probably the millionth time that night and forced myself to stand up straight.

When I'd scoped this place out earlier, it had seemed like leather was the main thing everyone was wearing. So, not wanting to stand out (in a bad way, at least), I'd spent most of yesterday night scouring the mall for the perfect outfit to make my girl bar debut. In the end, I'd settled on a pair of black pants that were a lot snugger than I was used to, but I was doing my best to ignore how tightly they squeezed my butt and how the leather around my thighs made a swishing sound every time I took a step. I liked the way they looked paired with the platform boots and lacy top I'd picked out, and I wasn't about to start second guessing myself now. I had an image to develop, dang it, and this ensemble was my first real attempt at a look that said "cute, ready to party, but also classy and maybe just a little bit scary?"

Judging by the appreciative heckling and wolf whistles from the women standing outside smoking that I passed on my way into the bar proper, it seemed to be working. Which was good, because I was starving.

Well, okay, not, like, *starving,* starving. I'd had a snack a couple nights back. Still, I was hungry, it was Friday, and this girl bar just off campus was chock full of tasty temptations. And I do mean that both figuratively and literally, hehe. If only my parents could see me now. Alcohol *and* wanton same sex attraction? They'd crap a brick!

Assuming they didn't die of a heart attack from the whole "turns out vampires are totally real and I'm one of them now" thing, that is.

But, yeah, point is tonight was going to be special. I was going to pick up a girl! Like, for real. No more fretting about perdition and temple recommends (pretty sure I'm not allowed in there anymore anyway), no more swiping on apps and chickening out on messaging every time I got a match. It was high time I started living my best unlife, and that meant kicking my way out of the closet and never looking back. Me and whoever I clicked with tonight were going to laugh, dance, hopefully have some nice noncommittal make outs, and then, before the sun rose, I'd sink my fangs into her neck and drink my fill.

That was the plan, at any rate. I actually had to meet someone first before I could put it into action, though.

Okay, okay, okay. Don't freak out, you can do this!

You'd think that after literally dying and being reborn as an unholy, bloodsucking creature of darkness a few months ago that this would be easier, but noooo. Even with the ability to bench press a car and shift through shadows at will, it turns out you can't just undo two decades worth of chronic anxiety, body image issues, and good, old-fashioned conservative brainwashing. I'd tried self-help books, motivational YouTube speakers, and even (don't judge me, okay?) a $400 course on how to kiss. And, yes, I know that makes it sound like I'm a skeevy pick-up artist, but I'm really not, I swear.

"Oh dear."

All right, I'd made it inside. That was good. There was also a *lot* more aggressive hip grinding and boob grabbing than I'd been anticipating, but that was totally fine too. Like, for real. Definitely not intimidating at all. I was a gosh darn vampire for crying out loud! A literal queen of seduction and shadow and all that other spooky crap. I wasn't about to let a bunch of kind of scary lesbians with cool piercings and wandering hands scare *me* off!

"Hey there, sugar lips, haven't seen you 'round here before," drawled a woman with intricate snake tattoos slithering their way from her trim waist all the way up to her neck (I knew for sure, because she wasn't wearing anything underneath her half-open leather vest).

"I'm new!" I all but yelped, not sure if she could hear me over the way too loud dance music.

"I love me a cut of fresh meat," she replied (still not sure if she could actually hear me or not), as she reached out and pawed at my chest. "Mmmm, *nice*."

"Ah! Um! Um...!"

Dang it! Maybe I should have gone to that stupid piano bar after all? No, no! I told myself I wanted to find someone tough and exciting tonight, and I wasn't going to get that with a bunch of nerds pretending to be fancy. Still...

"Oh! Hey, there's my friend!" Not waiting for Miss Grab-by-Hands to respond, I made a beeline toward the first opening in the crowd I saw. "Um, sorry, gotta go. Bye!"

Swallowing down the mouthful of bats trying to escape my roiling stomach, I misted away into an out of the way corner as soon as I was lost amid the press of people, and then forced myself to take several long, deep breaths before I had a panic attack. Granted, I didn't actually need to breathe anymore, it was kind of just a habit at that point, but the act of inhaling through my nose, holding it for a five count, and then letting it out through pursed lips helped to settle some of my frayed nerves.

I was *not* going to bail.

Cycling through some more only kind of, sort of helping breathing exercises, I succumbed to the bone-deep need to start moving again before anyone noticed me. And, locking onto the glint of a cluster of golden earrings from across the bar, I soon found myself closing in on a woman in dark gray jeans and a snug, sleeveless top that showed off an extremely well-defined pair of olive-toned biceps. Besides making *extremely* good use of whatever gym membership she had, she looked like she was probably somewhere in her mid-to-late twenties, with severe features, and a head of shaggy brown hair cropped short on the sides and long enough on top to run your fingers through while you admired the subtle shade of eyeshadow she'd picked out for the evening.

My mouth began to water just looking at her, while my brain exploded into fight or flight mode.

Crap, crap, crap! What do I do? What do I do? Do I offer to buy her a drink? Do I just buy her a drink and then offer it to her? Wait, is that even really a thing, or is that just what they do in movies? Oh gosh, oh no, um... um...!

Look. Shut up. I was new to this, all right?

I'd thought that my first attempt at flirting would be with someone mousy who liked video games and maybe hated going to bars like this since they were apparently full of way too many really pretty butch ladies who seemed ready to eat you alive if you let your guard down. Not, you know...

Her.

Should I just go? Maybe I should just go? Frick! No, I can't just go, not yet! I have to at least try to talk to her, don't I? Agh! YouTube made this look so much easier.

Objectively, I understood there was no real reason to be as intimidated by this woman as I was. She was just sitting there, alone as far as I could tell, leaning with one elbow against the bar while she scrolled through her phone and occasionally took a pull from her beer. Even so, there was no denying that something about her laconic, utterly self-assured mannerisms had my undead heart stuttering to a halt inside my chest and the little hairs on the back of my neck standing on end. The flashing lights from the dance floor were painting her strong profile in alternating shades of red, green, and blue, and I found myself just standing there like an idiot, mesmerized by the way the corners of her mouth would occasionally quirk up into a half-smile while the labyrinth of veins beneath the elegant column of her neck continued to pump away at some truly knee-wobblingly delicious O negative.

Dang it, dang it, dang it! I knew I should have asked Chloe to come with me. She's good at this sort of stuff. Crap!

She still hadn't noticed I was there. Natural stealth was definitely a perk for a vampire with social anxiety. I could still bail. All I had to do was drift back into the crowd and try my luck with someone else, or else maybe mist up onto the roof and go fleeing back to my apartment. Instead, though, I bit the inside of my cheek, clenched my flip-flopping stomach extra tight, and reached out to tap her on the elbow.

It was now or never.

"Um, hi!"

Morgan

"Hmm?"

The tentative caress of chilly fingers across my arm sent a shiver up my spine as I rounded on the most adorable baby goth I'd ever seen with an aborted growl caught halfway in the back of my throat. I hadn't scented her approach, but her gentle timbre and unsure, halting manner managed to soothe my irritation at her for breaching my personal space uninvited.

"Hey there, cutie."

Cutie was absolutely the right word for her, I mused, as I got my first proper look at her. She was plump in all the right places, with midnight black hair that framed her shyly smiling face perfectly. Her black nose ring dully reflected the strobing light from the dance floor, drawing my attention away from her tight and vaguely Victorian top (which was totally at odds with her equally tight pants) and up to a pair of startlingly blue eyes circled by rings of dark eyeshadow that seemed to make them all the more vibrant, especially with how crazy pale she was.

Damn. Those were a great shade on her. Bright and clear, and just a bit startling. Like jumping into a lake in the middle of winter.

"I'm Melody!" she yelled over the music, yanking me away from my swim through her eyes with a start as her pale face flushed a hot shade of pink. "Melody Harper!"

Melody, huh? That seemed appropriate given how easily her voice was on the ear.

"Morgan," I replied, taking full advantage of our height difference (even with those boots she was wobbling in, she was a total shorty) to force her to tilt back her head and expose her throat so that she could meet my eye. "Morgan Bloodfang."

"Oh! Um, nice!"

Oh god. "Nice?" Seriously? Could she be any more nervous? Usually when people heard my edgelordy ass last name, they'd at least demand to know if I was being serious or not. Still, her nervousness, like everything else about her, was pretty cute. Especially when it made her nibble on her lower lip like that.

"Let me guess." Cocking a brow, I watched in silent amusement as she fidgeted in front of me like she was waiting for permission to go to the bathroom. "Fresh out the closet?"

"Um... Pretty much, yeah."

Melody's smile shifted from nervous to a chagrined sort of flirty then, and I found myself giving her another once-over. Oh yes, those hips were totally doing it for me. Round, soft, and just *begging* for a squeeze. Or ten. I bet she'd look great bending over, maybe with those pants around her ankles and that fat ass-

Down, girl. Don't go breeding her before you've even had a drink together, I chided myself, shaking my head to clear it before my mind could run off any further with that particular mental image.

Thankfully, Melody didn't seem to have noticed. She was way too busy ogling my chest while trying to seem like she wasn't ogling my chest to pay much attention to anything else.

"So, uh, how'd you know I'd just come out?" she asked after taking a second to lick her lips, reaching up and brushing some of that silky smooth hair behind an ear.

It immediately fell back into place, and I felt a muscle in my cheek twitch.

"Please, honey. You look like a rabbit who just realized she wandered into a den of wolves."

At least one wolf, anyway.

I hit her with my most seductive grin, letting my teeth sharpen to points. Humans never seemed to pick up on the teeth, but part of them always started to squirm whenever they came out to play, and Melody was no exception.

"Oh, well. That's, uh... That makes sense. I guess..."

Some of the tension eased out of her exposed shoulders then as she seemed to gather her courage.

Good girl.

"This is my first time at a bar too, actually."

Awww. She really was a baby goth!

"No shit?" Guiding her around to the empty stool beside me with my Doc Marten (Dani had run off with that sophomore in the short skirt, so it wasn't like she needed it anymore), I grinned. "Too young to drink, or are you one of those girls who gets all wild and crazy after half a beer?"

"No, I'm old enough. Just... I used to be Mormon is all."

Well now, that was a new one.

"Wait, Mormon? Like, John Smith and magic underwear, Mormon?"

This time she was the one to grin.

"It's actually *Joseph* Smith, but, yep, that's the one."

"Heh. Aren't you guys not allowed to drink?" I teased, adopting Melody's own halting cadence as I leaned in and added in a breathy whisper against her ear. "Or, um… you know… kiss girls?"

"That's definitely a big no-no!" The color in the shorter girl's cheeks deepened to a lovely dark pink as she stiffened on her stool. "But, I um... I've kinda recently left the church."

"You don't say?"

"Yep!" Her shoulders drew back with obvious pride as she nodded. "I'm officially a daughter of perdition."

"My, my, how very sinful, you naughty thing, you."

I winked, and was rewarded with a shy smile for my efforts.

"That's me all right."

She absently scratched at her nose ring as she broke off eye contact, shifting it over half an inch.

Awww, of course it's fake.

"Guess you could say I'm making up for lost time worshiping a god I don't believe in anymore." She rolled her eyes at that. "Oof, that sounds so melodramatic. I promise I'm not a Reddit atheist debate lord. I'm just done with church is all."

"Oh, I don't know… I can think of some things you could still do on your knees, sweet cheeks."

Oops. Stop it, Morgan. Quit eye-fucking the girl you literally just met.

"Uh, so…" My momentary hesitation seemed to help Melody relax a bit more, though it didn't do anything to ease the tomato flush in her crazy smooth cheeks. "Twenty-one and still a freshman, huh? You *are* a freshman, right?"

She definitely had big fresh from home energy, that was for sure.

Again, she nodded.

"You a bit of a late bloomer then, I take it?"

"Basically." Melody did an admirable job of hiding her chagrin behind leaning over to catch the bartender's eye with a little wave. "I spent a year living at home after high school, then went on a mission for a year and a half to Brazil, and then worked at a movie theater for a while after that before deciding that being an usher wasn't actually my life's calling."

"You don't say?"

Cute and bilingual? Nice.

"Oh my *gosh*, yes!" she exploded in between ordering a drink of her own, which the bartender comped her for for whatever reason. Guess I wasn't the only one who thought she was cute. "If I never have to mop another sticky floor, it'll be too dang soon. I swear some people were spilling their drinks on purpose some nights."

"I'll bet you looked real good in your usher uniform, though," I teased. "I can see it now. Little vest and hat, and a way too short skirt that showed off those tasty thighs."

"You're good," she giggled, said tasty thighs pressing together self-consciously as she thanked the bartender for her drink before bringing it up to her lips and pretending to take a sip, almost but not quite managing to hide the way her nose wrinkled at the smell. "It was one of those fancy theaters with recliners and actual food and stuff. Our theme was 'golden age tinseltown'. Ugh. So lame."

God. She looked even cuter when she was pouting. It made me want to make her do it more.

"Awww, that sounds kinda fun, actually. What? Was the pay bad or something?" I pressed, taking a healthy pull from my own beer while gliding the inside of my left foot up her calf, making her shiver but not actually pull away. "I've heard servers in those places pull in mad tips."

"I mean, it kinda depends on the showing." Melody paused to lick her lips as her gaze once again fell back to my chest. The little horn dog was practically drooling! Church camp must've been an absolute nightmare for her closeted ass when she was younger. "Matinées didn't pay very much, but midnight releases were great. But, well…"

Again, her cheeks flushed bright as she busied herself with passing her drink from one hand to the other and back again.

"Oh come on, don't leave me hanging."

"It's silly."

"Okay, now I have to hear this. Out with it, before I *make* you tell me."

That last bit had been a bit of a gamble, but the way she'd jerked back with a half-choked squeak was definitely a good sign.

"Heh. Well, when you put it like that..." Melody's gaze drifted over to my right elbow as she gathered her thoughts. "I'm pretty sure I had bruises on my butt half the time when I woke up the next morning after those showings."

"Bruises?"

Well now, that was interesting.

"Drunk people like to pinch… and smack."

I'd just been in the middle of taking a swig from my beer to keep my own pinch-happy hands occupied, and had to fight back a spit take.

"Hey! Don't laugh! I'm serious!"

Okay, yeah, fuck it. I'm going in.

"Oh, I believe you," I coughed, scrubbing the back of my hand across my broadly beaming mouth before leaning in and grabbing a handful of delightfully soft cheek overhanging the back of her stool, making her squeak again. "Mmhmm, yep. I can see why you'd make such a tempting target."

"O-Oh yeah?"

Rather than panic or indignation, I could swear her startled eyes flashed *red* for a split-second, before her face lit up in a flirty smile that had me tightening my grip.

"Absolutely." My voice dipped down into a low growl as I dragged her in by that perfect ass so that I could brush the lightest of kisses against the corner of her mouth. "And I'll have you know that I'd love nothing more than to bend you over right here and now and send you straight to heaven, church girl."

"Um, well, um, uh..." Apparently, I'd managed to short-circuit her brain with that one. Not that I was complaining. Especially not when she buried her burning face against my shoulder. "Th-That could be fun."

Oh yeah, she was a total bottom.

Fucking. Score.

"You know, I used to hate my butt," I felt her mumble against my collarbones, trembling a little. She pulled back then and did her best to smile her way through her embarrassment as I finally let her go. "Recently, though, I've had to learn to just be okay with looking the way I do."

"Well, for what it's worth, I think you look great."

Toasting her with my beer, I drained the rest while watching her fidget adorably.

"Well, uh..." Again, she swept that swoop of black hair back behind her ear. And, again, it fell right back into place almost immediately. "You're not so bad yourself."

"Oh yeah?" Cocking half a grin at her, I dropped my empty bottle back down onto its coaster. "Why, Melody. If I didn't know any better, I'd say you were *flirting* with me."

"Maybe..." She looked up at me through her curtain of raven-dark hair, fluttering her eyelashes. "Is it working?"

"Definitely."

"Oh! Phew, that's good!"

"So, anything in particular that drew you to me?" I pressed, my grin turning unapologetically predatory. "I mean, I'm a total hottie, obviously, but it's still a pretty packed bar."

"Um..."

"Go on now," I ordered, putting just a hint of playful menace into my tone for no other reason than to watch her squirm some more. "I'm listening."

"I-" She swallowed, reached for her drink, thought better of it, and then blew out a little huff. "It's silly."

Awww, she was actually tongue-tied. Still, I wasn't about to let her off the hook that easily. I wanted my answer, and she was going to give it to me. So, I waited. Staring her down until she finally cracked.

It took all of three seconds.

"It was your earrings!" she blurted, spilling a bit of sticky sweet alcohol onto the bar.

"My earrings?"

Honestly, I was a little surprised she hadn't said my breasts. Lord knows she'd been staring at them long enough.

"Yep." Melody's smile this time was fragile, but undeniably genuine. "They make you look really pretty."

In a profound show of boldness (at least for her), she reached out and brushed her fingertips across my forearm. Her feather-light caress sent little shocks of electricity over my skin, making *me* shiver this time.

Two could play at that game, though.

"I bet you're even prettier under all those clothes," I purred (shut up, it's just a figure of speech), reaching out and brushing my knuckles along the gentle curve of her cheekbone, twisting a few stray locks of hair around a finger as I made a show of licking my lips. "Tasty too."

Melody looked like she was seriously considering making a break for the exit at that, having apparently reached the extent of her courage. I wasn't about to let that happen, though. I *needed* her beneath me tonight.

Leaning in so that we were practically nose to nose, I took a surreptitious sniff while tightening my grip on her hair just enough to bring her to heel. Beneath the floral aroma of her soap were hints of copper and... cupcakes? Yep, definitely cupcakes. Copper, cupcakes, and the unmistakable tang of lust. Actually, scratch that. It wasn't just a tang. She was straight up drenched in it.

Okay, yeah. I was absolutely going to devour her.

But, first...

"Hey, girl!"

My Second's raised voice snapped me and Melody out of our

mutual trance as she flounced over to us with her picks for the evening.

"Oooh. Who's your friend? She's cute!"

Ah, Dani. I love you. Best winglady around.

"Dani, Melody. Melody, Dani."

"Um, hi."

Disentangling herself from my hold on her hair, Melody half-turned with an awkward wave, but her smile hadn't dimmed. Which made my hackles rise just a little.

Dani, sensing my stirring displeasure flashed me a quizzical look, eyebrows arched. To which I nodded once, answering her unspoken question.

Yes, she was mine.

She just smiled right on back at me, making it clear she thought I was being ridiculous. Which, okay, maybe I was. But can you blame me?

"So, Melody," she crooned, sidling in behind her at the bar and not so subtly shifting her toward me with one foot on the crossbar of her stool. "You wanna come dancing with me and Morgan?"

"I-" Again, the girl looked like she was considering fleeing, but then visibly steeled herself. "I'd like that."

"Great!"

Clapping excitedly, Dani shoved her off of her stool and into my lap, for which I could have kissed her as I slipped my arms around Melody's waist to "steady" her.

"Come on, juicy booty," I chuckled, letting my hands wander down to give said booty another squeeze as I hoisted her up and started steering us toward the dance floor. "Let's see what you've got."

Melody

Oh. My. Gosh. I can't believe I hadn't done this sooner! Sure, things with Morgan were a bit scary at first, but we managed to push past that pretty quick. Even better, she thought I was cute! Which was good, since I thought she was totally gorgeous.

And not just because her carotid kept begging for me to bite it. (Though, that definitely helped.)

She was just so, so… *powerful.* I might be able to juggle SUVs like it's nothing, but my body was still soft and squishy and not in any way toned. She, on the other hand, was like steel wrapped in satin. Each sloping line and curve of her flawless figure a testament to the rippling muscles beneath. Then there was the way she'd just grabbed my butt at the bar. I mean, that was nice, albeit totally unexpected. I'd sort of assumed we'd maybe find a quiet corner to chat and possibly kiss and hold hands a little after a couple drinks, but I didn't mind her approach at all. In fact, I rather liked it. Like, a lot.

Like, a lot, a lot.

There was something about this random stranger taking control like she had, like I was hers to command, that was just…

Mmph!

The moment her hand had squeezed my cheek, my nipples had gone rock hard beneath my top and my panties had flooded with arousal. And now she was dancing with me.

Me!

Like, actually dancing too. None of that awkward, slow, one hand on the shoulder and the other held out to the side while leaving room for Jesus crap I'd been forced to smile my way through during church dances in high school. Oh no, Morgan was all grinding hips and possessive hands.

Lithe and quick, she moved us with an effortless grace that made me feel unwieldy and gangly by comparison. Not that it mattered. She was in complete control, and all I had to do was follow her lead and enjoy the music. I had no idea if I was doing any of this "right" or whatever (Was I pushing my butt into her too hard? Did she want me to arch my back so she could get at my breasts easier?), but that woodsy musk of hers mixed with just a hint of something spicy had me captive to her will, tightening my lower abdomen while my fangs ached for a taste of her.

One blissful eternity later, we both seemed to have had our fill of dancing. At least, Morgan had, judging by the way her chest was heaving and her chestnut hair was plastered with sweat to her forehead and neck. I hadn't broken a sweat, but we'd been all over each other enough that I don't think she noticed. Still, I did my best to pretend I was winded just in case. My heart was definitely pounding hard enough to sell it.

"Fuck."

Pulling me in roughly against her front, Morgan dragged me up onto my tiptoes with a hand on each of my cheeks, forcing me to tip back my head to meet her ravenous gaze before I went for that perfect throat.

"I want you. Now," she growled, her voice a low rumble vibrating into me where our breasts were pressed together.

"M-Me too…" I panted, licking my lips and just barely managing to keep my fangs in check.

Oh gosh, this was really going to happen, wasn't it?

Seeming to sense my hesitation, Morgan's fingernails dug ruthlessly into the seat of my pants (I swear I could feel them piercing the leather!), wringing out a moan from me as I tried desperately to grind my aching core against her.

"My bike's just outside," she murmured, teeth nipping at my ear, very nearly making me come there and then as I trembled in her arms. "We can be back at my place in five."

"W… Works for me, let's-" Shuddering, I sank my teeth into my lower lip, drawing blood with the tips of my fangs as Morgan shoved a steel-cored thigh between my legs, grinding the inseam of my pants against my sopping pussy. "Oh god!"

The words left my mouth without me even flinching at taking the lord's name in vain, and then we were kissing. Oh gosh, kissing her was really nice. Her mouth was wide and warm and seemed to know just what I needed as she led me through my first kiss with silent direction.

It was… She tasted like heaven. I'm talking top tier Celestial Kingdom, second anointing and all.

It was *amazing*.

"Let's go."

Morgan's order was just as compelling as my thrall right then as she hauled me up so that my legs were wrapped around her waist while she guided us off the dance floor, moving us toward the exit while shouting something to her roommate as we swept past her and the trio of women she'd drawn to herself. I was too busy fighting the twin urges to writhe against Morgan's washboard abs and to feed with reckless abandon to really pay attention to Dani's reply, but it had the cadence of an "Okay, see you soon!" sort of thing.

The crisp, autumn night air hit us like a sledgehammer as we stumbled laughing and sloppily kissing out into the Jackalope's parking lot. Morgan's hands were all over me, and mine were all over her. Honestly, if I wasn't so horny, I'd be genuinely proud of how bold I was being just then. I'm pretty sure that if I'd still had my temple recommend, it would've burst into flames right about the same time Morgan's teeth bit down against where my neck met my shoulder. The Law of Chastity had definitely gone out the window a long time ago.

I gasped and let out a little giggle as she backed me roughly up against someone's car, much to the amusement of the women smoking a few yards behind us. I didn't have much time to think about their leering grins, though, because just then Morgan was in the process of undoing the clasp on the front of my pants and slipping her hand inside my panties.

"You like that?" she huffed, grinding the heel of her palm against my clit.

"I- I-!"

"Answer me," she snapped, parting my slit with a finger and teasing at my opening. Her voice was rough and full of need, and I wanted nothing more than to listen to it for forever.

Well, almost nothing.

As soon as she started working a finger inside of me, I lost all control. My eyes flooded crimson, and my gaze bored into her amber eyes with a sudden deluge of vampiric compulsion that had her freezing one knuckle deep.

"Alley. N-Now."

My voice was breathy and strained, but my thrall was undeniable. And, bleary-eyed and listless, Morgan stumbled back and began staggering toward where I'd pointed.

I didn't wait to see if anyone else was watching us. I just misted into the alleyway ahead of her, my eyes burning in the darkness as I beckoned her deeper into the shadows and over to an out of the way spot behind a convenient dumpster. Not exactly the most romantic of places, true. But, hey, a girl has needs, and I was about to come undone if I didn't do this now.

As soon as we were out of sight (or close enough for it not to matter), I pushed her up against the bricks, wrenched her head to the side, and sank my fangs deep into her throat. Instantly, my mouth flooded with hot, life-giving blood. Sweet as could be, and pulsing with an intangible electricity that lit me up from the inside out like a supernova. While I drank, Morgan's body seized up, going stiff. Whatever chemical compound my fangs injected into my meals flooded her system with a blissful haze that made her forget all about the desperately horny vampire latched onto her neck as she was swept away in a deluge of back-to-back orgasms.

Massaging her artery with my tongue, I coaxed more and more blood out of her. It was just *so* good. Hands down the best I'd ever tasted. But, as I continued to drink, it began to dawn on me that something was wrong. My head was growing fuzzy, sounds around me were dulling, and sparklers of color were exploding behind my half-lidded eyes. That, and my entire body had suddenly grown heavy and weak. It wasn't exactly a bad sensation, but…

Oh crap!

I had to stop, like, now, but I was already losing consciousness.

If I didn't do something quick, I was going to pass out and Morgan was going to bleed to death on top of me.

No, no, no!

Marshaling what little energy I still had left, I rasped my tongue against the razor point of one of my fangs and lapped at the taller girl's puncture wounds, closing them in an instant with my blood.

Phew! Crisis averted.

Well, sort of.

With a quiet whimper, I let us both slump down the wall until I was collapsed on the ground with my head pillowed on top of her thighs while she lolled back against the bricks.

I had no idea what she'd think when she came out of my thrall, but…

I…

CHAPTER 2

Morgan

"The… fuck?"

Shit. Where was I?

Scratch that. Why did it smell like blood and rotten takeout?

"Oh."

Because I was leaning against a dumpster.

As for the blood thing…

"Shit!"

Melody was on top of me, and she was covered in blood from her mouth to halfway down her stupid, cute, lacy top.

"Oh fuck, oh shit."

This wasn't good.

Moving as fast as my way too heavy limbs would allow, I pressed my fingers to her neck and was relieved to feel a pulse. It was a lot slower than it should be and her skin felt like it was about ten degrees cooler than the chilly night air could account for, but she was still alive at least.

Okay. Seriously. What the fuck happened?

Did someone roofie us?

Hell, I wasn't even sure if I *could* be roofied. Benefits of a supernaturally-augmented metabolism and all that. Still, my arms and legs were totally drained, and my head was fuzzy. Not exactly the bad kind of fuzzy, mind you, but, yeah. Weirdly enough, it felt a lot like I'd just gotten fucked. Like, crazy good. I still had all my clothes on, though, and so did Melody, so I don't think anyone did anything to us.

Still…

This was definitely one of those "not good" types of situations.

"Hey."

I gave her shoulders a shake, jostling her bejeweled bat earrings.

She didn't stir.

"Hey, wake up," I repeated, layering some steel on top of my voice without thinking about it as I gave her a firmer shove.

It didn't wake her up, but it did manage to knock loose her fake nose ring.

"Mmmm… Pine cones…"

"Uh, pine cones?"

Instead of answering my question, she rolled over onto her back, drooling. It was honestly kind of cute. Except for the whole, you know, "blood all down her front in a dirty alleyway" thing.

"Morgan! There you are! I was- Oh shit!"

Thank fucking god.

"Dani!"

I was still flat on my ass leaning against my little intersection of brick and dumpster, cradling my raven-haired get's head in my lap.

"I'm all right," I reassured her with a drowsy wave, before letting my leaden arm flop back down onto the ground beside me. "Mostly. Feel like I need a nap, or maybe a quick shift, but that's about it."

"Okay…"

Dani didn't exactly sound convinced. Normally, I'd have been annoyed by her mothering, but I was too exhausted to care just then.

"So, what the fuck happened? You and Mel get a little rougher than you planned on? She looks like she's got one hell of a nose-bleed going."

"Good question. I'm not really sure," I admitted, grimacing as I brushed my fingertips along her neck in a half-hearted attempt to clean her up.

On instinct, I brought my wet digits up to my nose and sniffed.

"What the?"

I sniffed again.

"What's up?" prompted Dani, squatting down next to me and Melody and fishing out some make up wipes from her purse.

"This is *my* blood."

"Wait. Seriously?"

Reaching out, I let Dani get a whiff.

"Fuck. Yep. That's definitely you."

She started swabbing at Melody's face then. Wiping away the crusting blood and thin rivulet of drool leaking out of one corner of her mouth.

"So, uh... What happened? You don't *seem* like you're fountaining blood anywhere. Well, not anymore."

She gestured to my right shoulder.

"Pretty sure that top is ruined, though."

"Yeah... I don't know." I let my head drop back against the cold bricks behind me and tried to think. It was definitely harder than it should have been. "I... We were in the parking lot, I remember that. I had her up against a car, we were kissing, I'd just gotten a hand down her pants, and then... I woke up here."

Dani's glossy lips pursed in consternation as she started working her way down Melody's neck, and I felt a growl start to rumble up inside my chest as she reached her chest.

Covered in my blood or not, she was still mine.

My second just rolled her eyes, though, and drew back her hand.

"Yes, yes, Alpha," she soothed, half-mocking as she leaned in for a quick cheek nuzzle.

"Fuck off," I grumbled back with a playful smirk, nipping at her ear.

"Anyway, what do you want to do with her? She seems pretty out of it."

"I'd say maybe take her to a hospital, but her being covered in blood is a kind of a bad look, and the last thing I need is any of this getting back to my mom."

"God, tell me about it. She'd shit a brick."

I couldn't help but snort at that particular visual.

"Yeah, no. She seems okay enough for now. Let's just get her back to the house and let her sleep off whatever this is. That'll give me a chance to figure out what the fuck her deal is too. Something is definitely off here and I want to know what."

"Works for me."

Shrugging, Dani moved to help me sit Melody up, before slipping an arm around her shoulders while I did the same with her other side on slightly less stable legs.

"Ugh. Do we still have that steak in the fridge?"

"We do," Dani's look was simultaneously dubious and concerned as she looked me over again, her lips pinching into a worried line. "Seriously, girl. You sure you're doing all right?"

"Just feeling a bit weak," I reassured her, my inner wolf rankling at the admission. "I'll be fine after I've had something to eat and a shower."

"You sure?" My Second was clearly still worried. Which was one of the many reasons why she'd earned that position. I needed someone watching my back who gave a shit. "I could call Dorian and have her bring the Jeep, you know."

"No, no, that's fine," I huffed, lurching forward and doing my best to ignore Melody's sleep babble and tantalizing scent. Even unconscious, all I wanted was to ravish those delectable curves.

"Come on, let's get the fuck out of here. A walk sounds like just the thing right about now."

Melody

Some indeterminate amount of time later, the swirling colors and impossible shapes I'd been drowning in for who knows how long started to clear, and the world came back into focus. Only problem was, it definitely wasn't my ceiling I was staring at when I finally came to. For starters, it didn't have my cute string of bat lights from Halloween.

"Umph…"

Consciousness was still a battle, I was finding, and my limbs felt leaden and were slow to respond. Still, I managed to muster up enough energy to roll (well, more like flop, but whatever) over.

And immediately locked eyes with Morgan.

"Oh. Uh, hey…"

"Hey yourself."

Blinking languidly, I tried to claw away the last vestiges of… sleep? Blood coma?

Whatever you wanted to call it, this was definitely not good, and my brain, jerk that it was, was refusing to cooperate.

Morgan had changed in the interim between me discovering just how tasty her neck was and me (mostly) regaining my faculties. She was now wearing a pair of flannel pajama bottoms and a camisole. Under which, I couldn't help but notice with a fresh stirring of lust, a pair of hard nipples were tenting out the stretch cotton. Those, more than anything, gave me the energy I needed to sit up and turn to properly face her.

"So…?"

"So."

Again, she just repeated the word, legs crossed beneath her as she sat facing me in a swivel chair on the other side of the room.

I lost our impromptu staring contest after only a few seconds, looking away and noticing the window behind me for the first time. Or, more specifically, the very unwelcome gray tinge of sunrise peeking in through the edges of the (thankfully drawn) blinds.

Oh crap.

Actually, no. Not crap.

This was very much a *shit* sort of situation.

On instinct, I tried to will myself to disappear back to my apartment. Social awkwardness and lingering confusion be danged.

It didn't work.

It was too late.

I was stuck.

You know what? Screw not swearing. My parents weren't here to hear me anyway.

Shit fuck!

"How're you feeling?"

Morgan's question drew me back to the present with an unpleasant lurch.

Shit and fuck and double damn it.

Hey, this was kind of fun!

"I'm… fine, I guess? Bit sleepy."

"Glad to hear it. You were pretty out of it for a while there," she replied, still not giving anything away with her expression. "Do you have any idea what happened?"

"Happened?"

"I woke up in an alley behind the Jackalope with you covered in my blood and passed out on top of me."

"Oh."

"Oh?"

"Oh! Uh... That's weird!"

"Weird?"

Morgan cocked one perfectly plucked eyebrow at me. My lack of surprise was definitely not doing me any favors, and the coolly questioning look in her amber eyes was ratcheting up my anxiety by about a million percent. So, I did what I always did whenever I'd been (mostly) busted doing my best to fly under the radar. I lied as fast as I could!

"Well, I mean, *yeah*," I huffed, pouring just a touch of exasperated disdain into my voice. "Like, how could that have even happened?"

"That's what I'm trying to figure out," she reminded me.

"Oh, uh, right. Um, well..."

Ugh! Would it kill her to let the whole Law and Order SVU interrogator mask slip for just, like, a second?

"Maybe those drinks were stronger than we thought?" I suggested, trying not to grin as a brilliant explanation came to me in a flash of inspiration. After all, the easiest way to sell a lie is to basically just tell the truth selectively, right? "I'm still pretty new to alcohol in general and maybe that bartender accidentally gave us some really hard stuff on accident?"

"Oh yeah, one beer will tooootally knock you on your ass," deadpanned Morgan. "Actually, come to think of it, did you even *drink* any of yours?"

"Of course I did!"

"What'd it taste like then?"

"Uh... bread?"

"Honey. You ordered a wine cooler."

Crap! Was that what that was? How the heck was I supposed to know? It was dark in there and it came in a bottle! Besides, I was sort of busy staring at that little patch of freckles just over her carotid and-

"Okay, so, let's say you *did* get super-duper Mormon drunk on that wine cooler you didn't actually drink. How about all the blood?"

You know. I was starting to get the impression that Morgan was messing with me. Still, I couldn't just back down now. Not when I literally had my back against the wall and nowhere to run.

"I'm waiting."

"Uh..."

Crap, shoot, frick!

"Nosebleed?"

Before the word had even finished leaving my mouth, Morgan was out of her chair and crossing the room with the sort of loping, liquid grace that tightened my nipples beneath my slightly crusty top. Even trapped in some random girl's bedroom having to come up with excuses on the fly for why I'd been sucking on her neck in the middle of an alleyway, I couldn't stop my vampiric nature from rearing its stupid, horny head. I didn't have much time to be annoyed with myself, though. Because, the next thing I knew, she was on top of me. Shoving me roughly onto my back as she straddled my hips.

"All right, who the fuck sent you?" she snarled, digging the tip of a wicked looking knife against where I was pretty sure my heart was with one hand, while the other closed around my throat.

"Sent me?" I managed to squeak around her grip.

Wow, she was strong!

"You think I can't spot a goddamn assassin when I see one, bitch?"

Huh? Assassin? Seriously?

"I'm not-" I wheezed, fighting the near overwhelming urge to send her flying across the room.

She might have been way more muscular than I was, but I was still the one with the supernatural strength here. If I wasn't careful, I could really hurt her.

In response to my halting attempt at a denial, Morgan dug the tip of her knife (dagger?) even harder into my chest, piercing my top and the bra beneath and drawing a thin rivulet of blood from a shallow cut that healed a few heartbeats later.

"W-Wait!" I begged, prying her constricting fingers up enough from around my neck to get the words out around through trembling lips.

My vision went dim around the edges as I was rocked by a visceral sense memory that took the rest of my breath away.

Suddenly, I was back in that grimy alleyway last semester. Drowning in panic and flailing denial of the inevitability of what was going to happen while hard gravel dug into my bruised and bloody face as what little remained of my young, woefully underlived life spilled out from between where my fingers tried and failed to keep the hemorrhaging slits in my abdomen pressed together.

"P… Please!"

Why wasn't it working? You were supposed to apply pressure to cuts, weren't you? Sure, I'd gotten stabbed, but that was just, like, a bigger cut wasn't it?

A sob racked me then, hot tears draining away even more of the liquid that was supposed to stay inside of me.

This was so unfair!

I was doing everything I was supposed to, and it still wasn't working! I'd been praying frantically over and over again, begging for Heavenly Father or Jesus or the Holy Ghost, or heck, maybe one of those freaking Three Nephite jerks who were supposed to be wandering the earth changing flat tires and sharing the gospel to come help me out. Even so, no light above the brightness of the noonday sun shone down into that empty, nighttime alley, and no perfectly resurrected being of god made flesh appeared before me to ease my suffering.

It was just me, the stench of my own blood and urine, and the hot tears aggravating the cuts on my face.

"M-Morgan, I… I..."

This wasn't real.

This couldn't be happening.

I'd done everything I was supposed to! I was wearing my garments, wasn't I? They made me look like a gross albino potato and ruined so many outfits, but I stuck to them because I was supposed to, and they weren't doing anything. Weren't they supposed to be a protection against the evil deeds of wicked men or whatever? My mission president had told us all that story about the elders who'd been shot by muggers but somehow walked away with only bruises on their chests, hadn't he?

How come they got the miracle treatment and I didn't?!

Was I not worthy? Was I not pure enough?

I'd never acted on my same sex attraction, had I? I'd always recited the articles of faith forwards and backwards whenever impure thoughts started to creep their way into my head, and even confessed to my bishop (at least that one time) about how I'd looked at porn when I was a sophomore in high school. I'd repented, hadn't I?

This was all so *stupid*!

Maybe if I was a boy I'd be able to heal myself with a priesthood blessing. I know you're supposed to have two elders for that sort of thing, but if you could use Doritos for sacrament when you didn't have bread, couldn't you bless yourself in an emergency?

I just…

I didn't want to die.

"Please!"

With a hoarse, gasping wheeze, my eyes shot open and I resurfaced from the midst of the full blown PTSD flashback I was having enough to croak the word. Hyperventilating despite the vise grip around my neck, my trembling drew fresh blood from the tip of the blade digging into my chest, and my hands clawed desperately at my stomach for stab wounds that weren't actually there.

"I'm not an assassin."

"Okay, then what the fuck are you?"

Morgan's tone had softened somewhat, but she kept her knife right where it was.

"I'm… I'm…" I stuttered, tears clouding the fierce, still beautiful despite everything face above me.

My options were pretty limited here. I guess I could *try* and thrall her again, but that would require me to actually have full control of myself, which was a lot easier said than done just then. Plus, the sun was already well and truly up. Even if I'd been able to use them, most of my powers would be significantly dulled or totally ineffective until sundown. So, it was either boot Morgan off of me hard enough that she got knocked out for, like, twelve hours (which I was pretty sure was brain damage territory), or come clean. Regardless of what I decided to do, I was stuck here until sundown, and that knife wasn't going anywhere until I gave her what she wanted.

"I-" Swallowing around Morgan's gripping fingers, hot tears cutting zigzag patterns down my unnaturally pale cheeks and absolutely ruining my makeup, I admitted what I was to someone else for the first time ever. "I'm a vampire."

In an effort to head off the whole "are you serious?" back and forth that I was sure was about to follow, I opened my mouth wide enough for my fangs to come fully into view.

"So?"

To her credit, Morgan didn't seem even the slightest bit freaked out by this. But, she also didn't ease up.

"So..." I echoed, feeling suddenly at a loss for words, her unexpected reaction tempering my anxiety with confusion.

"Just because you're a vampire doesn't mean you're not an assassin," she clarified, lips twitching slightly.

"But... but... but I'm not!"

I guess she had a point there.

I could feel my panic starting to shift into exasperation now as fresh tears of frustration (rather than soul-rending hysteria) dribbled down to join their fellows on the comforter beneath me.

"I just wanted to meet a pretty girl and maybe make out!" I confessed, face flushing crimson as my words came out far whinier than I'd intended for them to. "I've been trying to work up the nerve to do this for *months*, and... and... Ugh! I totally screwed it up!"

That was the understatement of the century, but it still felt good to get the words out anyway now that I'd committed to the whole honesty thing.

Loosing an absolutely totally over it growl of frustration, I slammed my balled up fists against the mattress to either side of me hard enough to make us both bounce up an inch or two.

Which, miracle of miracles, caused Morgan's scowl to snap up into a sardonic smirk as she eased her grip on my neck and drew back her knife enough so that it was no longer digging into me.

"'Make out' in this case meaning using me as your personal juice box?" she prompted, her voice now a lilting tease that made my still hammering heart flutter excitedly.

"I mean…"

Looking away from her, my fangs dimpled the soft skin of my lower lip as I tried to think of something to say.

"I was only going to take a pint at the end of the night," I admitted in a humiliated mumble, staring unseeingly to my side at a poster she had up on the wall. "You'd have been fine after some cookies and OJ."

At Morgan's derisive snort, I rounded my head back to glare at her. After the emotional roller coaster she'd just dragged me through, I was getting pretty tired of her crap.

"Hey! It's not *my* fault you were feeling me up like that in the parking lot."

"Awww, what's the matter?" she crooned, not the least bit intimidated by my scowl, even with the fangs. "Are my fingers really that good?"

"Um, kinda," I replied around a pout without thinking, before clamping my lips together before they could let any more embarrassing admissions out. "Look, don't go flattering yourself. It's, like, a vampire thing, all right?"

"Uh-huh." Morgan's tone had shifted from taunting to bemused and genuinely curious. "And how's that, exactly?"

"Well…"

Suddenly, I was all too aware of the weight of her hips against mine. Her strong thighs straddling my waist, bleeding their warmth into me through the thin material of her pajama bottoms.

"Answer me, vampire," she ordered not unkindly, underscoring her command by gliding the tip of her blade in a small circle around where my left nipple strained for attention through the material of my bra and top.

The sensation of that razor tip had me trembling and my thighs squirming in an effort not to grind my groin into her.

"I… It's hard to explain."

"Try anyway."

It wasn't a request, and I found myself obeying immediately.

"Well, um, like, when I, uh… woke up? Was turned? Whatever you want to call it. When it happened, one of the things I noticed right away was that I had, like, a *way* more intense sense of touch. And, um-"

This time my hips did buck against hers, tilting the edges of her smirk up just a bit further in the process.

"Yes?"

"I… Okay, so, um, feeding is a, uh… It's sort of a sex thing," I admitted while my face did its best to burst into flames. "I mean, I have to eat to live, but it's also tied to arousal. And, um... when I bite people… I, uh… I kinda make them come. Like, a lot."

"Awww, look at you all hot and bothered."

Rather than be scandalized by this information, Morgan's face split into a predatory grin that looked completely natural on her. And, licking her lips, she glided the thumb of her free hand down along the hollow of my throat in a possessive caress.

"N-No I'm not!" I tried to insist, sounding way more defensive than I meant to.

At which point, Morgan's head tipped back and she loosed a straight up cackle.

"Oh… Oh my god! I get it now. You really *are* a virgin!"

"I-!"

"You are, aren't you? Oh god, that's rich. Here you are all horny and super sensitive all the time, and you haven't even gotten laid before."

"All right, fine! I was the perfect little closeted Molly Mormon and you were my first kiss. There. Are you happy now?"

"Awww, I do enjoy popping a cute girl's cherry," Morgan cooed. "Even if it's just her mouth."

The way she phrased that screamed double entendre, and did absolutely nothing to help with the whole being *extremely* hot and bothered thing I was dealing with just then.

"Anyway, I'd say I'd give you an A for effort, but…" Morgan sent her knife spinning away behind her with a casual flick of her wrist, apparently satisfied that I wasn't just an extremely aroused assassin. "You blowing your vampire load like that kinda derailed your hopes for getting fucked by a hot upperclassmen just a bit, didn't it?"

"Sh-Shut up! I said make out, not… that."

Much as I wanted to deny what she was saying, the humiliated squeak my voice had become made it abundantly clear that she'd hit the coffin nail right on the head. I'd definitely wanted her to take me in the parking lot.

"*Excuse me?!*"

That, apparently, had been the absolute wrong thing to say. The next thing I knew, Morgan had a fistful of my hair squeezed tight and was yanking on it hard enough to make me gasp as she brought her face down so that we were nose to nose.

"Don't go trying to get cute with me, you little brat," she snapped. "I'm still plenty pissed about that alleyway bullshit you pulled."

"Ow! Okay, okay! Geez!"

Again, I could've easily shoved her away, but I didn't want to lose a hunk of my hair in the process. Plus, well, there was no denying what this commanding shift in her demeanor was doing to me. I hadn't had enough relationship experience to definitively say if I had a "type" since I'd spent the last decade or so focusing on "not acting on my same sex attraction", but I was rapidly coming realize that strong, commanding women who could've once kicked my butt might just be it.

As if reading my mind, a smug half-grin returned to Morgan's tantalizingly close lips.

"The words you're looking for are, 'sorry, ma'am'."

She accompanied that suggestion (order?) with another yank.

"Ah! Okay, I'm sorry, ma'am!" I hissed, head rising up off of the mattress behind me in an attempt to ease the pressure on my hair.

Which just so happened to bring my lips into contact with hers.

"Mmph!"

Oh my gosh! Oh crap!

They were still so soft… and warm…

I was just about to pull back so I could apologize (I may be a bloodsucking monster, but I'm not *gross*. I don't just go kissing people without their permission!), when her grip on my head shifted to the back of my neck and she pulled me in closer, shoving her tongue inside my mouth with a satisfied growl.

Oh gosh, she tasted even better than I remembered.

Don't bite her tongue, don't bite her tongue, don't bite her tongue.

I very nearly lost it right there and then when her free hand slipped back inside my still unbuttoned pants and cupped my pussy through my once again soaked panties. Instead, an involuntary rumble of primal need emanated from deep inside of me as my hips rose up to grind against the friction her palm was providing.

"You want me, don't you, vampire?"

Morgan's voice was barely more than a murmur, but I heard her just fine.

When I only rolled my hips beneath her in reply, she moved her grip from the back of my neck down to paw at one of my hyper-sensitive breasts, finding its erect nipple through the material of my top and bra and pinching hard.

Crying out, my back arched as spasms of pain and pleasure jolted through me.

"Y-Yes, ma'am!"

"Wow, you weren't kidding about being extra sensitive to touch, were you? I'm barely even pinching you."

Morgan kept on rolling my nipple between her thumb and

forefinger while toying with my slit for a few more blissful seconds, seeming to revel in my whimpers and breathy gasps before releasing my breast and groin with a self-satisfied chuckle.

"You… You know I could kick your butt if I… If I felt like it, don't you?"

My voice was little more than a panting mess, but I managed to underscore my point by grabbing her by the hips and lifting her several inches into the air without so much as a grunt of effort.

"So?" she countered with a shrug, her voice a mixture of amusement and unshakable confidence as I held her aloft.

"So, I mean..."

Tipping forward without warning, Morgan snapped her jaws down onto the exposed junction where my shoulder met my neck, biting *hard*. Not enough to draw blood, but I still let her go with a startled yelp. She didn't ease her grip on me as her groin bounced against mine, though. Instead, she clamped down even harder with her teeth as I writhed beneath her, forgetting all about my vampiric strength as my fists bunched themselves up in her sheets and I moaned her name.

And then came.

And came *hard*.

"Ooooh fuh-rick!"

Crying out loud enough to surely wake the dead, my entire body was racked by an orgasm so powerful that it had me forgetting to breathe as I trembled beneath the warm weight of Morgan's body. Tides of pleasure ripped through me from where she had my shoulder trapped, ricocheting and gathering speed as my toes curled and uncurled in time with my spasming inner walls.

It. Was. Incredible.

Eventually, as I lay there with my chest heaving once again and my shoulder throbbing, my erstwhile meal at last let me go and rolled over onto her back beside me on the bed.

As she lay there, also breathing hard, I wanted to say something to her. Thank you, maybe? We'd definitely gotten sidetracked, that was for sure, but... it was just so late. I could feel the sun climbing ever higher toward its zenith. And, with each passing moment, fatigue was closing in around me.

I had to rest.

I...

Morgan

Holy shit.

I hadn't come that hard in... Well, to be honest, I don't even remember. Which was especially wild considering, you know, usually someone had to be touching my pussy to make me orgasm.

Still.

Definitely no complaints here.

Slightly more concerning, however, was the fact that my bite didn't seem to be healing. Normally that would make sense, but Melody was a vampire, and it had shifted from raw and red on her porcelain skin to the typical mottled purples and fading yellows of an older bruise.

"Uh-oh."

I hadn't *meant* to claim her, I really hadn't. I was just trying to teach her a lesson about who was in charge. But, well, here we were. One moment I was getting ready to fuck her, and the next I'd given her a mate bite. Maybe it wouldn't stick? She was a vampire, after all. Were their bodies even compatible with werewolf mate bites?

I could already scent our pheromones starting to mingle together where I'd bitten her, so chances were pretty good that they were.

"Well, shit."

Actually, you know what? Fuck it. This was a problem for future Morgan to worry about. It had felt like the right move at the time, and even now as I levered myself up into a sitting position and glided my fingertips along the marks I'd left behind on that decadently soft skin of Melody's, I couldn't bring myself to feel bad about it. She was mine. I had known that ever since the moment I'd first laid eyes on her back at the bar.

Still.

I guess I should probably ask *her* how she's feeling about me before I start making any plans to breed her. I mean, she was definitely into me, that much was obvious. And, like, if it stuck, that meant that on an instinctual level, at least, her body accepted my offer, right?

Agh! Stupid inner wolf. Why couldn't you just be cool and let me hook up with a cute freshman? Damn.

Again, though, future Morgan's problem, not mine.

In the meantime, I needed to figure out what to do with the girl beside me. I doubted I could just kick her out at this point. (Not that I particularly wanted to.) The sun was up, and I was pretty sure that wasn't something vampires were a fan of.

"Uh, Melody?"

She didn't respond.

"Hey." I know I'd rocked her world and all, I could smell her cum through her clothes and had felt her orgasming while she'd been writhing beneath me. But, even so, I hadn't made her come *that* hard, had I? "You all right?"

Giving her a little shake did absolutely nothing. Her eyes were closed, her face was serene, and-

"Oh fuck!"

She wasn't breathing.

I was back on top of her in an instant and just in the process of pinching her nose closed to start CPR, when I remembered what she was.

"Oh, right. Hmmm..."

I'd never actually met a vampire before, but I'd at least heard others in the pack mention them from time to time while growing up. So, following a hunch, I pressed a pair of fingertips to the side of her neck. Her skin was a lot colder than a normal human's should be, but I could still tell that her heart was (barely) pumping.

"Phew!"

She wasn't dead. Well, she was, but not, like, *dead* dead. She was just sleeping. Hibernating? In repose? I'd have to ask her what she called it once the sun went down again.

"All right, okay, let's just-"

Grunting, I wriggled and shoved her largely inanimate body into the corner where my bed met the wall, making enough room for me to lie down next to her beneath the covers. It was pretty late / early after all, and I was fucking exhausted from dancing and the multiple orgasms I'd been hit with while Melody had been chomping on me. Oh, and all the blood she'd helped herself to as well. Thank god I didn't have any classes today.

Stifling a yawn, I pawed for my phone where it lay on my nightstand, shooting a quick text off to Dani letting her know that Melody and I were all right and that I'd fill her in on everything after I'd gotten some sleep, before then setting an alarm for a few hours from now. My Second and I had some things to figure out before our impromptu house guest arose from her slumber.

"Don't think you're out of the woods yet," I snickered, snuggling up against Melody's soft, slightly chilly curves beneath the blankets. "I'm still going to get you back, you brat."

She didn't respond, of course, but I still pressed a kiss to her cheek. I couldn't help it. She was my mate, after all.

God, training her was going to be *so* much fun. Assuming she didn't tear me limb from limb, that is. Which, if I was being totally honest with myself, just made the prospect all the more exciting.

After all, who doesn't love a challenge?

CHAPTER 3

Morgan

As I was getting dressed later that afternoon, surprisingly well-rested given the circumstances surrounding how late I'd gotten to bed, there came a knock at my bedroom door.

"It's open!"

"Hey, girl, how's our mystery assassin doing?" Dani asked, poking her head inside and making a comical show of scanning for bloodstains and battle damage. "You two kill each other, or what?"

"Yeah, might've missed the mark on that one by just a bit," I conceded with a rueful shake of my head.

"And the understatement of the year goes to..."

"Okay, okay, get 'em all out now while I'm in a good mood. What else you got, bitch?"

Visibly perking up as she skipped over to my side with a perfectly-executed pirouette, Dani's teasing grin grew downright sadistic as she threw a look toward where Melody still lay curled up beneath the covers.

"Let's see, I worked out a whole tight five on how the easiest way to knock an Alpha on her ass is to be the least threatening freshman I've ever seen. Would you like me to start with that, or the limerick about the baby goth who huffed and puffed and blew you behind a dumpster?"

"All right," I laughed. "That's a good one."

"Thanks!" Beaming now, Dani turned her attention back to my bed and its snoozing occupant. "Soooo...?"

Joining her by the bed, I gave her a nonplussed shrug and then reached down to push back Melody's upper lip, exposing a pair of pearly white fangs.

"Vampire."

"Ah. Okay, yeah, no, that makes sense." Dani's lips pursed in thought as she went on. "I take it she's not the dangerous kind of vampire then?"

"You tell me."

Unable to hold back my smirk, I reached further down and gave one of Melody's nipples a sharp tweak through her shirt.

"Mmmm, buttermilk..."

And Dani completely melted.

"Awww! Can we keep her?"

"I hope so," I sighed, tugging aside the bloodstained collar on Melody's shirt to reveal the crescent moon of teeth marks standing out in stark relief against her eerily pale skin. "Otherwise, this is going to be pretty damn awkward."

"Oh." Dani, ever swift on the uptake, looked in disbelief from my mate bite, to me, and back again as she hissed in a breath. "Shit."

"Yeah." Stalling for time, I took a moment to smooth back Melody's raven-dark hair from her forehead. God, it was so soft. I could play with it for hours. "It kinda just, you know... happened."

"And?"

"And..." I tossed my hands up in exasperation. "And then she passed out from sun drain, or whatever vampires call it."

"So, wait, she doesn't even know that you've marked her? Morgan!"

"I know, I know!" I growled, annoyed at myself and annoyed that I had no right to be annoyed with Dani for her totally justified indignation.

Just because my bite seemed to have taken, that didn't mean Melody would actually want to see it through. And, much as I would have loved to just make that decision for her, I knew I had to be better than that if we were going to make this work.

Fuck, being responsible sucked sometimes.

"You don't have to say it, all right? I know what I did was reckless."

"That's certainly one way of putting it," agreed Dani with a truly astonishing amount of side-eye, crossing her arms over her chest in a way too good imitation of her mom's go-to move whenever she was about to tear one of us a new one.

"Look, you weren't there!" Working my thumbs into my temples, I tried to push back the stress headache that had been hounding me ever since I woke up. "You weren't feeling what we were when I had her beneath me after she'd come clean. Even if it *was* a stupid move, and I'm not saying it wasn't, in that moment, it was still the right decision."

"Fair enough." Reaching out, Dani gave the nape of my neck a reassuring squeeze before leaning in for a quick nuzzle, helping to ground my swirling emotions with some much-needed skin-to-skin contact. "Guess we'll just have to wait and see how this all plays out, yeah?"

"Yep, pretty much," I agreed with a sigh. I hated waiting. "Thanks, Dani."

"Any time." Crossing her arms, Dani swapped out her stern but supportive second in command scowl for a sly, knowing grin as our gazes simultaneously wandered back to Melody and her luscious curves. "Soooo… You two fuck or what?"

"Heh. Almost."

"Almost?!" Dani's voice shot up a full octave in comical

disbelief as she jabbed a disbelieving finger toward my sleeping mate, as if I was somehow unaware of the crazy good catch I'd managed to land last night. "How do you *almost* fuck a hottie like her?"

"Well..." I deliberately kept her waiting as I blew out a breath that lifted my bangs off my forehead. "Turns out that Hot Topic Carmilla here is a straight up, capital V virgin."

"Shut up!"

"I'm serious! I made her come just with my bite, and then she passed out like she'd been hit by a freight train."

The sun might've had something to do with that, but I wasn't about to share that particular detail if I didn't have to. I had an image to maintain, after all.

"Oh my god." Dani's jaw dropped in shocked delight. "That. Is. Adorable!"

"I know, right?" Grinning right back at her, I took a second to smooth the covers over my sweet Melody before striding toward the door. "Now, come on, quit ogling my mate and let's go bug Dorian about something to eat. Turns out that heavy blood loss can make you pretty damn hungry. We can figure out what to do with sleeping beauty once the sun goes down."

Melody

"Excuse me, do you know time it is?"

It was such a simple question, how could I not answer?

"Yeah, it's-"

But, of course, he doesn't really care. He just wants me distracted so he can punch me in the face and push me into that alley.

He shoves me against a wall hard enough to knock my breath out as his hand closes around my throat, freezing me in place I can even reach up to try and staunch the blood dribbling out of my nose.

Oh gosh, is it broken?

"Give me all your shit," he hisses, pressing the tip of a knife against my stomach.

Wait. Is this really happening? This can't be real life. It can't be. Who just robs someone like this? No way is this real.

"Now, bitch!"

Okay, that knife is real. It's really sharp, and really hard, and has me sucking in my stomach when he pushes it in just a bit deeper.

"I'm not gonna tell you again!"

I should have just given him what he wanted. But I just had to decide now was the time to grow a spine. And, of course, all those YouTube self-defense lessons aren't worth anything the moment he starts stabbing me.

"Oh fuck, oh fuck!"

That's right… You... better… run…

Cold... It's so cold…

I thought dying was supposed to be all warm and fuzzy at the end…?

What a rip off…

How long have I been here...?

Why hasn't anyone called an ambulance yet...?

Crunching on gravel, and then a pair of shoes…

Heels?

"Oh, you poor thing," she clucks. She sounds like she's just found me crying over a skinned knee, not bleeding to death in a puddle of garbage water and my own urine. "Here, let me help."

She's squatting down…

I like her stockings…

Something starts dribbling against my mouth. Of course it would start raining now. Typical.

Well, at least things don't hurt anymore. I guess it could be worse.

Rolling over, I stretched my arms above my head and let out a nice, long yawn.

"Mmmm..."

I have to say, there really isn't anything quite like the gentle caress of a full moon to wake you up in the evening. It's a million times better than a blaring alarm clock, that's for sure.

Only problem was, I wasn't at home.

"Crap!"

With one panicked thought, I was misting back onto my feet in the middle of Morgan's bedroom. Thankfully, I was alone just then, but I could still hear the steady *thump-thump, thump -thump, thump -thump* of multiple healthy hearts beating somewhere inside the house I was in. I mean, I was pretty sure it was a house. It was way nicer than my apartment, at least. Either way, this was a certified *Not Good*™ situation, and now that I wasn't blood drunk and fighting back sun fatigue, things were suddenly looking about a million times worse than I'd remembered.

"Did she seriously bite me? What the heck? Who even does that?"

Like you're one to talk.

Shut up, brain.

Wait, no, don't shut up! Think!

All right, I was alone in a stranger's bedroom who knew exactly what I was, check. I'd totally ruined any chance I'd had of seeing her ever again when I'd- What had she called it? Oh, right, "blown my vampire load," check. And, my heart was hammering at about a million miles an hour, check.

Ugh. So much for being the smooth and charming seductress of the night.

"Hey, at least I didn't wake up with a stake through the heart. That's got to count for something, right?"

Truth be told, I wasn't so sure that a stake could actually do anything to me. While I'd discovered I had a crazy fast rate of healing after being turned, I hadn't put that particular aspect of my newfound powers through any sort of rigorous stress-testing. Getting stabbed to death once was more than enough for me, thanks.

"Okay, okay, okay."

Pacing circles around the plush rug in the middle of Morgan's surprisingly spacious bedroom (rich parents, maybe?), I tried to get my bearings

"Still alive. Sort of."

Despite my dire situation, I couldn't help a little smirk at my vampire dad joke. Look, cut some slack, I was only human… once.

"Not on my way to a secret government research facility or in handcuffs, either, so… I guess she didn't call the cops? Cool, cool, cool."

My pacing started to pick up its, well, pace.

"What the heck am I supposed to do now, though?"

Where was Morgan? Was she hiding from me? She had to be, right? Crazy good chemistry or no, I'd still come clean about sucking her blood without her permission right before passing out in her bed. If that wasn't a deal-breaker, I don't know what is.

"Okay, let's just-"

Misting over to her bedroom door, I gave the handle an experimental jiggle.

It wasn't locked.

"Why would it be locked? It's a bedroom door, not a prison."

Okay, so, no cops, no spooky government spies, no locked door, but Morgan definitely must be freaked out by the crazy vampire she left napping in her bedroom. Should I try and find wherever she was hiding and apologize? Maybe see if I could explain things better? Thank her for letting me crash? Would that just freak her out more?

Probably.

"Hey, gee thanks for the blood and the bed! I had a really fun time dancing last night. Can I get your number?"

Yeah, no. Definitely not.

"Ugh, this *sucks*!"

Growing more and more frustrated with this whole stupid situation, I stomped my foot without thinking, making the open laptop on the desk jump.

"Shi-oot!"

As if on cue, there came the steady tread of rapidly approaching footfalls out in the hallway.

"Crap, crap, crap!"

I could tell it was her. Even with a couple inches of hollow core door between us, I could still pick up faint hints of spice and pine trees. Gosh, she still smelled really nice.

"Hey, Melody? You up?"

The doorknob started to turn, and I freaked.

Look, I'm not proud of it, all right? Suddenly my heart was in my throat and my stomach was trying to escape through my feet, and I just... panicked.

"Oh! Um, I-!"

The door swung open, and boom, there she was. Fully dressed, and looking just *so* pretty. Her amber eyes had these little flecks of gold in them that were just-

"Sorry!"

And then I disappeared.

Morgan

"Uh..."

If there was any doubt left that Melody was what she claimed to be, that sudden puff of black mist as she vanished into literal thin air more or less sealed the deal. Along with sinking any hopes I might have had of easing her into the idea of being my mate.

"Well, shit."

"Problem?" leaning around the doorframe, Dani's eyes narrowed in confusion at my apparently empty bedroom.

"Looks like she bailed."

I shrugged, trying to hide my disappointment. Dani wasn't fooled.

"Awww, I'm sorry, girl," she soothed, hugging me tight and nuzzling me with her cheek. It helped to take some of the edge off the razors rolling around inside my stomach.

"Thanks," I sighed, dragging a hand through my hair as I took in a deep breath, trying to capture as much of Melody's copper and cupcakes scent as I could.

"Soooo..." my Second eventually prodded once I'd had my moment to mourn, her lips pulling back into a predatory grin. "We going after her, or what?"

Oh, Dani, never change.

"Do you even have to ask?" Scoffing with something approximating my usual self-assured, Alpha swagger, I spun on my heel and went storming toward the stairs. "Call the girls, we're leaving in five."

Melody

It took me less than ten seconds to flee back to my crappy bedroom in my crappy apartment with its crappy cinder block walls and crappy carpet and crappy blackout curtains and its crappy desk and it's-

Okay, deep breaths. Deep… breaths…

"I… I…!"

Or start sobbing. That works too.

The next thing I knew, I was out of my stupid pants, and my

stupid, crusty top, and my stupid bra and panties, and was collapsing face down onto my bed, groaning into my pillows while I kicked my bare feet against the mattress behind me in a good, old-fashioned temper tantrum.

Oh, great, I'd left my boots at Morgan's

Awesome. It wasn't like I really liked those or anything.

Snatching up one of my pillows, I buried my face in it and screamed.

"FUUUUCK!"

Sadly, swearing wasn't really helping anything, and after a whole bunch more foot kicking that also didn't make things any better, it finally hit me just how badly I'd screwed myself over. My night with Morgan had been absolutely amazing, and terrifying, and thrilling, and-

"Dang it, dang it, dang it!"

Letting out a distinctly inhuman growl of frustration, I hurled my pillow at my closet, knocking one of its sliding doors off its tracks and sending my snoozing cat scrambling for cover.

"Sorry, Momo."

Great, now my cat was mad at me *and* I didn't have my favorite pillow.

"UGH!"

Of freaking course the first time I really hit it off with a girl, I mess it up by going all fangs out after a little (really awesome) making out. Even worse, now I couldn't even show my face at the Jackalope again. Morgan was almost certainly a regular there, and even if I managed to get her alone long enough to thrall her into forgetting everything that had happened between the two of us, she'd probably already still told all of her friends about the psycho freshman who bit her in the parking lot.

Oh crap! Are vampire hunters a real thing? I mean, vampires obviously are, so it stands to reason…

You know what? Screw it. I'd worry about that later. For now, I just wanted to cry, and that's exactly what I was going to do.

Operation Let's Kiss a Pretty Girl had been an absolute

disaster, and all I could do now was tuck my tail between my legs (shut up, I don't have a good bat idiom for that one) and pretend that I hadn't spent the most amazing night of my unlife with someone I could never see again. That her strong hands hadn't made me swoon. That when she laughed, my stomach didn't tumble over and over as I watched her cheeks develop the most beautiful pair of dimples. That her blood didn't taste like the purest-

"Gosh freaking dang it."

Wracked by fresh, self-loathing sobs that reduced me to a blubbering mess, I yanked my comforter up over my head and curled into a ball beneath it. Never more than now did I wish I had someone I could talk to about all this crap. Awkward dates and (admittedly, self-inflicted) heartbreak were all things my mom was supposed to be there for, but that was a total nonstarter. I was in so many closets with my parents at this point that I was finding Christmas presents they'd forgotten about from fifth grade.

This was all such bullcrap!

Half-blinded by tears, I misted out of bed and onto the floor with a harrumph and started clawing at my inside-out pants for my phone. Maybe I could get Mom to help if I just switched up the pronouns and didn't mention the whole "met at a bar" thing? Except, shocker of all shockers, my phone wasn't in my pants. I must have left *that* at Morgan's too.

"Of freaking course. Why wouldn't I have?"

Rolling over onto my back, I flopped out onto my mattress with another puff of black mist.

"Forget it, Mel... Just forget it," I tried telling myself through clenched teeth before I could explode from pure frustration and disappointment. "Just take a nap and everything will look better when you wake up."

They probably wouldn't, but it was either that or start on the homework I'd been putting off, and the last thing I wanted to do just then was explain in one thousand words or less how important Generally Accepted Accounting Principles were. So, blowing out a distinctly undignified huff through my clogged nostrils that definitely didn't dislodge an embarrassing amount of snot, I closed my eyes around a few more angry tears and willed myself to fall asleep despite having just woken up. Mostly just succeeding in summoning up a whole bunch of mental images and sense memories of the way too short time I'd had with Morgan.

Awesome. Thanks, brain.

"Humph."

Tis better to have loved and lost, my butt, I thought to myself with a scoff, unable to stop my lips from twitching up just a little. *Shakespeare is such a douche.*

CHAPTER 4

Melody

It took a few nights of good, old-fashioned moping before I felt like I'd more or less gotten that disaster of a near hookup out of my system, but I managed it. Honestly, I felt kind of silly now for how dramatic I'd been when I'd bailed on Morgan. Aside from her knowing I was a vampire and crashing on her bed without asking, things hadn't been *that* bad, had they? There was no way we could see each other again, sure, and I was still bummed that things had blown up so spectacularly between the two of us. But, hey, there were plenty more fish in the sea, right? Plenty of tall, muscular, confident, and intimidating fish who would just love to get their strong hands (fins?) all over me while we-

Er… Yeah.

Maybe I could give online dating another shot? I mean, I did just dye my hair and all.

While I'd been out picking up some wet food for my cat last night (and by "picking up", I mean shoplifting, because it's surprisingly fun and when you're an immortal being, money suddenly seems really stupid), I'd decided that a change of color was just what I needed to put that whole embarrassing incident at the Jackalope behind me. My shower looked like a murder scene now, but I was feeling pretty darn cute if I do say so myself.

I should totally take a new profile picture when I get home. Oh! I could do a whole photo shoot. That'd be fun!

Maybe I'd even take a couple naughty ones too while I was at it? (Just for me, obviously, shut up!) I was feeling a lot more confident about myself after having it so thoroughly confirmed for me that I was, in fact, attractive in the eyes of others. Before I could do any of that, though, I really needed to get something to eat.

"Brrrr! This is some bullcrap. How is there seriously nobody out right now?"

I'd been walking laps around the interconnected network of heavily-wooded jogging paths that wove around the outskirts of campus for the last half hour, hoping to find someone out and about who I could take a quick bite out of. But, so far, I'd been coming up empty. Granted, it was starting to get pretty cold at night now that Halloween was over, but there were usually still at least a *few* dedicated runners who could be relied upon to push through the uncomfortable weather to get their cardio in. At least, there had been the last time I'd gone hunting out here.

"On your left!"

Oh, hey, speak of the devil. Or, in this case, cute jogger. As I rounded a bend in the trail, a dark-skinned woman went speeding past me. Her heart was pumping away at the steady, measured pace of a veteran athlete, pushing some absolutely scrumptious B positive through her veins in a way that practically begged me to have a taste. Plus, well, she was decked out in this flattering (and scandalously formfitting) tracksuit that managed to stir up my lustlust as well as my bloodlust, and if that's not a happy meal, I don't know what is.

Hmmm, maybe I could try asking her out after I'm done? She'll definitely need a cup of coffee or something to replace what I took, and I can be charming! Morgan liked me, didn't she?

Ugh. Morgan.

Yeah, no, never mind. Forget that. No way, no how. Nope. I was done with in-person dating for at least a year. I was just going to grab a quick drink and then get back home to Momo, my fuzzy slippers, and the half gallon of Cookies and Cream I still had left while I continued laddering in Arcana the Hunting Online.

"All right, showtime!"

Blowing out a breath that failed to fog up in front of me like it would have back when I was alive, I took a second to get my game face on. Then, in the split-second between one step to the next, I misted from my spot some thirty feet behind my target and reappeared right in front of her with my hands raised up into spooky claws.

"Bleh- Oomph!"

Okay, so, I'd *planned* on startling her like a proper vampire (I am a night predator, after all), but instead I got a faceful of jogger boobs and we both went tumbling to the ground.

"Jesus! What the fuck?" my would-be snack started to demand from where she sat nursing a sore backside on the gravel in front of me.

She was staring at me with a lot more annoyance than fear for someone who'd just had a head-on collision with a vampire that had appeared out of thin air, but I guess she just figured I'd been trying to prank her by jumping out of the bushes or something. Either way, I was feeling like a total jerk for knocking her over like that.

"Sorry, sorry!" Springing back to my feet, I stooped down to hoist her up after me with my hands underneath her armpits, before just as quickly remembering what I was supposed to be doing as my stomach gave an audible rumble. "Oh, and for this too."

Before she could say anything, I scooched us off the trail and over to a suitable looking tree, which I then pinned her gently but firmly against the trunk of.

"Comfy? Nothing poking into your back?"

She looked like she was about ready to bite my head off, or maybe start screaming for help, so I adjusted my grip and clamped a hand over her mouth just in case. Which, I belatedly realized, forced me to mold pretty much every inch of my much shorter frame to hers in an extremely intimate embrace.

"Oh. Um. S-Sorry..."

Stammering like a total dork, the sensation of those exercise-warmed, muscular curves pressed so close to my much softer ones to the point that I could feel her pulse thumping into me, a powerful sense memory of Morgan doing the exact same thing last Friday ripped through me, and I had to fight my way through a sudden series of full-body shivers. Something which seemed to only further annoy my soon to be snack.

Oh my gosh, was she *growling* at me?

"Look, I promise I'm not going to hurt you," I tried to reassure her, wincing as soon as the words left my mouth. "Okay, that sounds really bad, but I'm serious. And, yes, before you say anything, I know that's *also* what a crazy serial killer would say to try and make you relax, but I swear I'm not a-"

Rather than further freaking out like I feared she would, my jogger just rolled her eyes and made a little "get on with it" gesture.

"Um, soooo, yeah," I forced myself to continue, now addressing a knot in the tree trunk just above and to the right of her head rather than those impatient amber eyes. "I'm just going to take, like, a pint or two. Fair warning, though, it's not an exact science given the extraction method, but I know what I'm doing and you'll be fine. Just, uh, you know, make sure you drink a lot of water tomorrow, and maybe eat some red meat too if you can?"

This time she huffed out a breath through her nostrils and mumbled something into my palm that sounded a lot like, "Seriously?"

"You, um… You haven't done this before have you?" I found myself asking, starting to feel like I was missing something super obvious. She just shook her head, though, and I shrugged. "Well, okay, if you say so."

At least I knew what I was doing for this next part. Carefully, I angled her head to the side to expose her pulse point, my eyes flooded crimson, and then my fangs pierced her carotid. I still had my hand over her mouth as that first rush of hot, coppery bliss splashed across my tongue, but me and my involuntary blood donor both still managed to let out twin sighs of satisfaction. Mine of a gnawing thirst finally being slaked, and her in a prolonged series of nonstop orgasms.

When I'd first started feeding after being turned, moved by a bone-deep thirst and primal instinct, I'd been worried I'd kill someone by accident. Fortunately, while it was definitely easy to get swept up in the sensation of someone's very life force flowing into you while they came and came beneath you, I also had apparently developed a rather acute sense of blood pressure. As a result, I was able to easily pick up when I'd at last crossed into that metaphorical danger zone with my jogger and knew that it was time to let her go before she was too drained to make it home safely. And so, with a reluctant huff through my nostrils, I nipped at my tongue with one of my fangs and used the resultant trickle of vampiric blood to seal her neck wounds before unclamping from her and licking her skin clean.

Waste not, want not, after all.

But, just as I was starting to feel pretty pleased with myself for such a (mostly) well-executed takedown and feeding, a pair of strong hands settled against my hips and pulled me in against an oddly familiar pelvis.

"Hey there, Carmilla. Deflower any virgins lately?"

Morgan

A very undignified (and absolutely adorable) choking sound escaped from my favorite vampire as I dug my fingernails in against her hips.

"Cheese and freaking crackers on a tuna fish sandwich!"

"Nope, just me," I laughed, holding her firmly in place as that juicy ass ground against my front with her startled squirming. She had on this snug pair of jogging pants that hugged her hips beautifully, and all I wanted to do just then was rip them off and see what she had on underneath.

"M-Morgan?"

"Mmhmm. Long time, no see, batty buns."

It had actually only been a few days, but I'd be lying if I said I hadn't been getting impatient. The girls and I had tracked Melody back to her apartment that very same night she'd disappeared on me, and I'd almost pounded down her door as soon as we figured out which unit she was in, intent on giving her a piece of my mind along with a dose of my belt. But, hearing her sobbing through her bedroom window had stopped me in my tracks, reminding me that I wasn't dealing with some obstinate submissive who should have known better than to defy her Alpha. No, Melody was special. And, clearly, was also processing some heavy emotions (I mean, I'd triggered the fuck out of her the night before with the whole holding her at knifepoint thing, hadn't I?), and I wasn't about to pile onto any of that just for a mildly pissed off booty call.

At least, not yet.

I could wait.

And, yeah, I know I could have just left her phone on her welcome mat, but I wasn't about to let her off the hook *that* easily. She was mine. There wasn't any doubt about that, not after what I'd done to her and the time we'd shared together. No. Now it was just a matter of when, not if, we'd meet again and she decided if she wanted me to be hers as well. Besides, it was nice to have an excuse to see her again that wasn't just me wanting to jump her vampire bones.

"What are-? Oh gosh," she panted, licking those ruby-stained, kissable lips. "What are you doing here?"

"Hmmm?"

Her breathy question pulled me back from my daydreaming about what her silky soft hair would feel like between my thighs, and I realized with a smirk that my hands had started to wander up her sides toward chest while I hadn't been paying attention.

"You never said goodbye." Guiding her away from where she had my slightly dizzy looking wolf backed up against a tree, I took the opportunity to finger a lock of her now crimson hair. "This is new."

"Wha-? Oh! Um, yeah, I did it last night."

Glowing with barely-suppressed excitement, Melody nestled more fully against me, settling into my sturdy frame like she knew she belonged there. Which, I'm sure the affection-starved vampire side of her did, even if her mortal brain hadn't quite caught up yet.

"It's called Vermilion Vortex. Do you, um… Do you like it?"

Smiling into that unruly mop of freshly-dyed hair, breathing in the wonderful mix of cherry conditioner, copper, and cupcakes I found there, I ground my already wet and stirring core against her ass. Making her gasp as her hips pushed back on reflex against me.

"Red suits you perfectly."

"Really? You don't think it's too much? Mom never let me-"

"Don't make me repeat myself." I shushed her with a playful nip at her earlobe.

"Eep!"

God, I wanted to make her cry out like that all fucking night.

"It looks great."

"I, um… Th-Thanks," Melody mumbled sheepishly, before tensing and hurriedly adding. "Not that I, like, did this for you or anything! I just thought-"

"Shhh…" I soothed, leaning in and placing a tender kiss to that same spot on her neck where she'd bitten me last Friday. A full body spasm rippled through her at the press of my warm lips to her frigid skin, and with a soft sigh like she was slipping into a hot bath after a long day, she collapsed into me, confirming that I'd been right on the money about claiming her for my own.

Clearly, we were made for each other.

"So, um, not that it's not really nice to see you again, but..." She took a moment to shift nervously on her unsteady feet, clearly conflicted about whether she should pull away from me or not as she no-doubt thought back to how we'd last parted.

"Yes...?"

I made the decision for her, tightening my grip around her waist. I wasn't about to let her go. Not that easily.

"How'd you even find me? Not to brag or anything, but I'm pretty good at sneaking around when I want to be." She nodded toward where Tatiana still stood dazed. "She certainly didn't see me coming, hehe."

"You rely way too much on that disappearing act of yours," I replied matter-of-factly, resisting the urge to scoff at my little vampire's puffed up ego. "You're not nearly so hard to track down as you might think. Hell, we've been able to follow you by your scent alone all week."

"My... scent?"

I could practically feel Melody's brows knitting together in confusion as her head tilted to the side, further exposing that throat of hers in an unconscious invitation for me to seize it between my jaws and-

"But I've been showering," she protested, snapping me back to reality with a snicker.

"I said scent, not BO, goofball. All I have to look for is that combo of blood, sex, and the wild lavender soap you like so much, and lo and behold, there you are."

"But-!"

"Hush."

Cutting her off again with a firm command and an even firmer squeeze, she obediently clamped her mouth shut with a suppressed squeak. God, that was a fun noise.

"Anyway, the girls and I thought we'd come say hello after we'd let you have some time to cool off from your little tantrum."

"It wasn't a tantrum-!" Melody immediately began to protest, just barely missing my foot with her outraged stomp (which was good, since I'm pretty sure she would have pancaked it), before the rest of what I'd said caught up with her. "Wait. What girls?"

"Hi, Mel!" chirped Dani, stepping out from around me with a little wave.

"Oh! Um, hi, Dani," my no doubt soon to be mate greeted nervously, stiffening in my arms as it finally seemed to dawn on her that she'd been well and truly ambushed. "Didn't see you there."

"I know, hon." Dani winked. "That's kind of the whole point of stalking prey."

"Ah. I, uh… I see."

"And you've already met Tatiana," I continued before my pouty vampire could protest that she wasn't prey, nodding toward where Dani was now helping the long-haired wolf stand up straight while she caught her breath.

"You… You were right," she panted. "Worked like… like a charm."

"Am I ever wrong, T? Thanks for playing bait, by the way."

At my shit-eating grin, she just rolled her eyes.

"No prob. Happy to… Happy to help," she said, starting to catch her second wind. "Though, I think I might need some Gatorade or something after that. I haven't come like that in a hot minute."

"Hear that, Dani?" I couldn't help but tease while Melody's face took on a shade of red not all that dissimilar to her hair. "Better step up your game."

"Pft, whatever," scoffed my Second, slapping her off and on again fuck buddy on her round ass with more force than was strictly necessary. "If I knew all it took to get you moaning like that was a little neck nibbling, I'd have done it a while ago."

Tatiana, capitulating to the reprimand with all the good grace of a true, dyed in the wool brat, kissed Dani's cheek.

"Bitch."

For which Dani gave her another hard ***SMACK!***

"Slut."

"Need anything else, boss?" Tatiana asked then, rubbing at her track pants while feigning a pout.

"Nope, I'm good for now. I'll see you both back at the house later."

"Works for me." Shrugging her lithe shoulders, Tatiana wrapped herself around Dani's arm and started dragging her back the way we'd come down the trail. "Come on, sugar tits. It's time to put up or shut up."

"Oh, if you insist..." came Dani's long suffering sigh before giggling as the two of them broke out into a loping run. "Bye, Morgan, bye, Mel! See you later!"

Melody

"Uh... Bye? I guess?"

The surreality of Morgan and her friends showing up out of nowhere was finally starting wear off enough for me to think straight again, but before I could round on the taller woman and demand to know what the heck was going on (or maybe just run away before she could call the cops on me for mauling her friend), she was reaching around and tucking something thin and rectangular into my front pocket.

"You forgot this back at my place," she said by way of explanation, patting my phone through the thin material of my joggers and momentarily short-circuiting my response with the way her fingers lingered over the elastic material of my waistband before pulling the loose knot I'd tied in the drawstring free. "Incidentally, you might want to call your mom back. She's been blowing you up all day about something called FHE and these guys named Elder."

"Oh, fuck me," I groaned, the profanity slipping out with surprising ease as I tipped my head back against a pair of extremely comfortable breasts in bone-deep exasperation.

Of freaking course. Count on the church to barge in and totally derail my post-feeding high and the fluttery excitement of seeing Morgan again by rearing its ugly, pious head. Very cool. Thanks, Mom. Love you too.

"I mean, sure, if you want." Morgan's low, velvety timbre had my toes curling inside my high-tops and the rest of me breaking out in shivers as she leered down at me, a devious smile playing at the corners of her mouth. The next thing I knew, I was being spun around and shoved up against the very same tree her friend (Tatiana?) had just abandoned. "What'll it be, cutie? Hands, mouth, or are you ready for the real deal?"

"I... I...!"

I'm pretty sure my undead heart exploded inside my chest from pure startled panic as she leaned in closer still, bringing that wide, grinning mouth of hers only a fraction of an inch away from my trembling lips.

"Then again, you might want to touch base with your mom first," she added in a husky murmur, tickling me with her breath as she wound a stray lock of my hair around a finger. "She seemed pretty worried."

"Yeah, w-well..."

Desperate to have something else to focus on other than the muscular thigh that had somehow found its way between my legs while I wasn't looking, I gritted my teeth and pressed down hard on that tender spot of guilt and resentment inside myself that had been festering away long before I'd ever become a vampire.

"I'll pass, thanks."

"Is that right?"

With the way Morgan's eyebrows quirked up, I'd swear she was impressed with my defiance. At least for a moment, anyway.

"I don't know if you've picked up on this yet, sweets, but I don't typically tolerate being told no," she crooned, those fierce eyes boring into me with enough predatory intensity to reduce my legs to jelly. (Good thing she was already propping me up, huh?) "So..."

She licked her lips, briefly revealing teeth that, now that I was hyper-fixating on anything and everything other than how good her bouncing knee felt against my rapidly-drenching groin, seemed far more pointed than they had been the last time I'd seen her.

"Explain yourself. Now."

"Er..."

"Well?"

Unwilling to surrender gracefully, but understanding on some instinctual level that I was thoroughly outclassed in both stubbornness and raw intimidation, I blew out a disgruntled harrumph through my nostrils and grumbled, "I haven't actually told my parents about leaving the church yet, okay?"

"Ahhh."

Immediately, Morgan's expression softened into something amused and sympathetic as she shifted from toying with my hair to stroking the slope of my cheekbone with the pad of her thumb.

"Or being gay?" she prompted, sounding almost gentle now.

"Um, yeah, that too."

"See? Now was that so hard?"

"No, not really…" I couldn't help but grin just a little bit with the admission. Morgan had this way of making it hard *not* to smile whenever she was pleased with me, I was finding. "Pretty sure they'd take me being a vampire way better than any of that other stuff, though."

"Oof, that's rough. I'm sorry you have to deal with that." Though succinct, I could tell that her words were genuine, and they (combined with the brief peck on the lips that accompanied them) helped buoy my spirits up higher than they had been in all week as she eased back from me enough to start steering us toward the jogging path in the opposite direction of where her friends had disappeared down. "Come on, let's go for a walk. I've missed you."

"Oh my gosh, really?"

"Mmhmm."

Yes, yes, yes!

Maybe I hadn't totally screwed things up after all?

"I, um, I've missed you too."

Morgan's hand dipped down from where it had circled around my waist to give my right cheek a firm squeeze through my pants as she chuckled.

"Good girl."

And, yep, there went my heart again.

"Th-Thanks!"

Suddenly all too aware of just how sloppily I was dressed, I surreptitiously attempted to finger-comb my freshly dyed hair into some semblance of order. I hadn't exactly planned on seeing anybody tonight, so I'd just gone out in a pair of ratty tennis shoes, comfy jogging pants, and an old band tee from high school. And, while that was all definitely comfortable, compared to Morgan and her pinstripe blouse, black jeans, rakishly coiffed hair, and cool leather bracelets, I felt like a total slob.

Still, she'd made all this effort to come find me, hadn't she? It wasn't like she would be expecting me to be dressed to the nines, right? Right?

Gosh, I hope so.

Eager to distract the taller girl from just how absolutely not put together I was right then (I hadn't even bothered with putting on a bra, for crying out loud!), I did my best to swallow my fluttering nerves and forced myself to keep talking. At this point, it wasn't like I had anything left to hide from her anyway, and she'd already shown that she could be considerate and gentle, so I figured I might as well just let it all out while I had the chance.

"My parents, they, uh… they've noticed that my faith has started to slip ever since I moved away and they can no longer drag me to church themselves. At first, they tried dropping lots of hints about wanting me to get more involved with the local ward here. You know, 'Oh hey, there's a dance next Saturday, maybe you'll meet a cute boy?', or 'Have you asked your relief society president what you should bring to the linger-longer yet?', stuff like that. Then, when that didn't magically get my butt back into the pews, they started taking the direct approach by calling my bishop and trying to get him to sick the missionaries on me, and I've just… been doing my to ignore it, I guess." Blowing out an exasperated huff, I gestured up and down at myself, smirking slightly. "Besides, even if I did try and talk to them about all of *this*, it's not like there's any sort of casual way to bring it up when you talk on the phone maybe once a week at most, you know?"

Morgan scoffed.

"Hey, Mom, how's the weather back home? Oh, by the way, turns out I like bumping clit and crosses make me hiss uncontrollably. Tell Dad I said hi and that I won't be back for Christmas!"

"Mormons don't do crosses," I reflexively corrected her, all the while succumbing to what felt like my first genuine giggle since last Friday.

"Whatever, smartass."

"Hehe, thanks! I *am* pretty smart aren't I?"

"Don't forget juicy." Again, Morgan's hand went for my butt, and this time I couldn't hold back a moan as she gave it a rough squeeze. "Oh yeah, definitely juicy."

Her fingers were like pure magic for my overactive sense of touch, and she had me melting against her as my steps faltered.

"Oops! Um, I-"

"Shhh…" Morgan cut off my bashful stuttering by nuzzling her cheek against mine before pressing a kiss to it as she strengthened her hold on my seat to keep me upright. "I've got you, babe. Just relax and let me take care of you, yeah?"

I swallowed my first couple responses that she didn't have to that, and that I didn't want to be a bother, and instead made myself nod against her, burrowing more fully into her reassuring warmth.

"All right. I… I can do that."

I think.

Again she kissed me, murmuring "good girl" into my ear and sending a giddy spasm of delight ripping through me yet again as my smile returned with a vengeance. For several long, blissful minutes after that, we just walked in silence. Lost in our own thoughts and enjoying the feel of one another in the crisp night air.

It was perfect.

"I'm sorry that your parents aren't there to support you like they should be," Morgan eventually said. "Knowing that your support system is hanging on by a thread must be really scary."

Her empathy and understanding put a giant crack in the shield I'd managed to raise between me and my feelings about my crappy parents, and I felt my chest start to tighten.

"Thanks," I mumbled, sniffling as stealthily as I could. I definitely didn't need to have her see me break down sobbing. *Again.* "And, yeah, it totally sucks."

Morgan's low chuckle at my unintentional vampire pun went a long way toward pushing back the rising tide of sorrow inside of me.

"Eternal life and godlike powers are at least a decent replacement for parental love and affection," I tried, earning myself a skeptical grunt and a sidelong glance as I continued to trace out the meandering line of my tangled thoughts. "I think I'm just realizing now that I've already accepted that my parents aren't going to magically be there for me like I was hoping they would. It… It hurts, but it's hurt for a while now, and it at least doesn't break me in half like it used to."

Morgan's lips quirked up into a smile that looked downright proud.

"I think you're a lot tougher than you give yourself credit for."

"Maybe you're right. At this point, I think I'm mostly just worried about what I'm going to do when they inevitably decide to cut me off. They've been paying my rent and tuition and everything else since I moved out here, you know."

"Would they seriously do that to you?" Once again, Morgan's grip tightened around my waist in a protective squeeze. "Just leave you high and dry because you weren't into chasing dick?"

"Oh, abso-freaking-lutely they would. It's called loving the sinner but hating the sin. After all, wickedness was never happiness, and they wouldn't be helping me make righteous choices as a daughter of our heavenly father if they continued to support me when I was so blatantly breaking the Law of Chastity."

"Okay, wow. That is some Grade A fundamentalist bullshit."

"You can sure say that again."

"That is some Grade A fundamentalist bullshit."

"Hah!"

Morgan's outrage and easy sense of humor were doing a lot to help me feel better about my impending financial doom.

"At least shoplifting as a vampire is pretty easy." Trying to emulate her seemingly boundless confidence, I tossed my hair and stood up just a bit straighter. "Fun too."

"I knew you were a naughty little sinner from the moment we met."

My fangs dimpled my lower lip in a shy smile at that.

"Yep, that's me. Straight up daughter of perdition right here."

"Hail Satan?"

In a moment of pure synchronicity, we both flashed each other devil horns while sticking out our tongues, and immediately dissolved into a fit of giggles so powerful that we very nearly went tumbling into a bush.

"Okay, but, yeah," I eventually managed to say once we'd gotten ourselves more or less back under control. "As nice as stealing is for keeping my cat fed and my wardrobe fresh, I can't exactly put my cell phone company's online payment portal under my thrall, which is a bit of a problem."

"Couldn't you just go to an actual store and get whoever is working there to mark your account as paid off?"

"Hmm, maaaaybe? I hadn't really thought of that before. But, even if I could, I'd still feel really bad. What if I got someone in trouble?" "You know, you're awfully considerate for someone who thinks of herself as a bloodsucking monster."

"But I *am* a-"

"Oh shush."

SMACK!

The unexpected ricochet of a hard palm against the seat of my pants had me jumping forward a full two steps as my face all but burst into flames. Fortunately, Morgan stopped me from saying something stupid by once again capturing my waist in the sturdy circle of her arm. Pulling me in against her in a sidelong hug as we started moving again.

"There's a whole world of difference between being a monster and acting like an asshole, you know."

"What do you mean?" I asked in a transparent attempt to deflect away from how hot and bothered that single swat had gotten me.

Morgan's reply was a disbelieving snort.

"Well, for starters, I can't help but notice that campus isn't littered with the corpses of cute coeds with neck punctures."

"Of course it isn't! I'd never-"

"Exactly," she cut me off with yet another quick peck to the cheek. "From what I saw between you and T earlier, I could tell that you were actively trying to avoid draining her dry. Thanks for that, by the way. Pretty sure her mom would be more than a little pissed at me if I let her only daughter die just so I could rope my would-be girlfriend into a surprise date."

I almost said, "You're welcome," before the rest of what she'd just said caught up with me and I had a brief heart attack. Date? *Girlfriend?!*

Oh my gosh, oh my gosh! I squealed internally, just barely managing to stop myself from dancing in place as I schooled my features into something that hopefully came across as nonchalant.

"Okay, so *maybe* you *might* have a point about how evil I may or may not be," I allowed, feeling proud of how steady my voice was as I said that. "But, would it change your opinion if I were to tell you that I'm seriously considering robbing a bank?"

"No shit? Never pegged you for the Ocean's Eleven type."

"Oh, don't get me wrong, I'm not planning on investing in a bunch of burlap sacks with dollar signs on them or anything," I hastened to reassure the bemused looking Morgan, my stomach flip-flopping pleasantly at the idea of her being impressed with me. "But, you've got to admit that having a huge pile of cash on hand would pretty much nip all of my money troubles in the bud."

"I'll admit I wouldn't mind nipping *you* in the bud."

"I- Um- I..."

I wasn't quite sure what she meant with that particular double entendre, but the way she said it filled me with a liquid heat that geysered up my neck even as it flooded straight between my legs. Gosh! How was she able to do that to me so easily? I know I was still a novice when it came to flirting and stuff, but I thought I'd at least be able to hold my own a little bit better this time around.

Thankfully, after what seemed like an eternity of me stuttering like a total dork, Morgan finally took pity on me enough to resume our conversation.

"So, what's stopping your big heist?"

"Um, mostly just that I don't have any idea how I'd do it without leaving behind a bunch of fingerprints or video footage or something. I really don't want to go to jail, cops still sort of scare me even if I am technically immortal, and there's no way in heck I'm going to live off the grid to evade the police. I like Netflix and roller rinks way too much."

"Roller rinks? Seriously?" Morgan's brassy alto took on a surprised note to it then. "What? Like, roller derby?"

"Oh my gosh, there's no way I'd ever survive a game with those ladies!" I laughed, forgetting for the moment that I was now fully capable of reducing a human being to a pasty smear if I felt like it. "No, no, I just like to skate and dance while they play music. It's fun!"

I felt Morgan's broad shoulders shrug, lightly jostling me against her chest in a way I didn't at all mind.

"Never been, but I'll take your word for it."

"We should go! I'll teach you how to skate if you don't know already. I promise you'll like it."

Holy crap, did I just ask her out on a date? Another date?

"Hmmm… Maybe. If I did, would that mean I get to see you in a cute sequin skirt and matching top?"

"Um, maybe?"

How does she know what my rink outfit looks like?

"Maybe, huh?"

"I…" Swallowing down my nervousness, I did my best to be bold. "I guess you'll just have to come along and find out, won't you?"

A contented sort of growling sound rumbled up from deep inside of Morgan's chest with that, its bassy timbre reverberating directly into clit as I swooned against her.

"Guess I will."

Was that… Was that a yes?

I think that was a yes!

Before I could work up the nerve to double-check with her, Morgan spoke again.

"Seriously, though, isn't financial support one of those things that your seethe is supposed to handle for you?"

"My what now?"

"Your seethe," she repeated, sounding just as confused as I did. "You know, your clan, your pack, your unholy cabal of leather-clad vampire buddies who happen to live in the area. Weren't you introduced to them by your sire?"

"What's a sire?"

"What do you *mean* 'what's a sire?'" Morgan's explosive disbelief made me jump, but her hold on my waist kept me right where I was. "Your sire is the person who fed you their blood and turned you into a vampire."

"Huh. Now that you mention it, I guess that lady did pour something into my mouth when she found me..."

"Right. Her blood."

"If you say so."

"Oh my god."

We'd reached a small sitting area at the end of one of the

path's branching segments, and Morgan brought us to a sudden halt between two concrete benches.

"You really have no idea what you are at all, do you?" she demanded, dragging me around to face her with an expression that looked uncomfortably like panic.

Still, her accusation hit way too close to home, and I found myself bristling as my lips pressed together into a stubborn scowl.

"And you do?"

Morgan just shook her head.

"A lot more than you do, apparently."

"So?" I hated how right she was and how scared that made me. "What's there to know? I suck blood, the sun gives me migraines, and I pretty much have a legal obligation to wear black nail polish. Big deal."

"Are you seriously copping an attitude with me right now?"

"Maybe I am. What of it?"

"Melody..." came Morgan's warning growl.

"Morgan..." came my mocking imitation of it.

Up until now, it had been so easy to ignore how totally out of my depth I was with this whole vampire thing. When I'd woken up in that alley just as the sun was starting to rise, I'd been so disoriented that I'd tapped into my newfound abilities without even realizing that was what I was doing, and had vanished across town and back to my bedroom inside my apartment. Even there with the blinds down, though, I could still feel the relentless pressure of the sun beating down on me, and I'd ended up cocooned inside my blankets beneath my bed (thank goodness for elevated college beds and their extra storage space) until it was night again. After that, the next few days were a total blur of panic and hunger, but by some small miracle I managed to avoid killing my roommate. Suffice it to say, I *thought* I'd had this all figured out by now, but Morgan had managed to bring all of those old anxieties right back to the surface.

"Look," I snapped, desperate to reassert myself, and once again regretting that I barely cracked five feet in the high-tops

I was wearing. "It's none of your business how I live my life, okay?"

"Sorry, not sorry, but actually, it totally is." Morgan's lips pulled back into a feral grin then that made me glad I had her hands holding me upright since it knocked my knees right out from under me. "You're mine now, which means your well-being is very much my concern."

That was... oddly sweet and reassuring, even if slightly alarming in its possessiveness. Well, alarming, and also really freaking hot. Like, dang. Still, I knew that her saying that should've ticked me off, and yet something about it just felt... right.

Like I *wanted* her to take charge and make sure everything was all right.

Like I *wanted* to belong to her.

Like it was meant to be.

Which meant that it was time for a change of subject as fast as humanly / vampirically possible.

"So, um, be honest with me. Are you, like, a magical karate nun or something? Is that why your blood messed me up so badly the other night, and why you and your friends were able to find me so easily?"

"Hmmm, maybe." Morgan's amber eyes flashed with amusement as she humored my fumbling attempt to distract her. "What if I was?"

"Well, for starters, it would make all that stuff I said about leaving the church feel really lame since apparently there'd be an actual god to be mad at me about it."

"True. Fortunately for you, I'm not a karate nun."

"Awww, bummer. That would've been fun."

"Sorry to disappoint, but I'm afraid I'm just a regular ol' werewolf."

"Ah, okay, cool- Wait, *what*?"

The force of my surprise sent me reeling backwards. But, again, Morgan's sturdy grip on my shoulders kept me right where

I was in front of her as she leered down at me with a toothy (perhaps, too toothy?) grin.

"Seriously?"

"Yep."

"So, like…?"

"If I hear you say Twilight, London, or awoo, I can promise you are not going to like what happens next, you little brat."

Ah. Okay, so no shirtless Morgans running through the woods then. Bummer.

"And none of that 'tie me up on the full moon so I don't hurt anyone' shit, either."

"So it's not, like, a monthly curse thing where you lose control and eat your friends?"

"I don't know, Melody, is *your* condition affected by garlic?"

All right, she had me there.

"Not really, no," I conceded, that strange sense of surreality washing over me once again, this time accompanied by a stirring of... what? Shame? Embarrassment? "Sorry if that was rude."

"Oh, pet, never apologize for not knowing something."

Um, pet?

Again, that probably shouldn't have made me shiver like it did, but there was no denying that coming from her, it made my stomach lurch like the first drop of a roller coaster while my face flushed hot enough to rival the sun.

My gaze had drifted down to the laces of my high-tops at some point without me realizing, but a pair of fingertips beneath my chin had my head tipping back up to meet Morgan's eyes as her grin turned downright feral.

"Besides, you were partially right."

She drew me in roughly against her then, dragging me up onto my tiptoes with a hand on either of my bottom cheeks, bringing us nose to nose as she made a show of licking her lips.

"I *do* enjoy eating my friends," she murmured against the corner of my mouth.

Oh gosh, I still had blood on my teeth, didn't I? Apparently, she didn't care, though, because the next thing I knew, she was kissing me and I was kissing her, and everything else suddenly didn't matter as I melted into her. Unlike her previous smooches tonight, this was anything but chaste as she worked her tongue in past my fangs to claim my mouth entirely.

"M-Morgan, I..."

Just like back at the Jackalope, my brain had gone completely to mush and all I could do was cling to her as my body swam with the twin needs to be held close and to be taken in any and every way possible she could think of.

Well, that, and to drink as much of her blood as I could.

"God, you sound so fucking hot when you're whimpering like that," she panted, her lips drawing back into something undeniably predatory as her eyes glowed golden in the muted orange of the sodium lamps. "Speaking of..."

CHAPTER 5

Morgan

Okay, shit, this needed to happen right fucking now or else I was going to shove Melody over one of these benches and take her there and then, pre-established game plan or not.

Jesus. Just the *thought* of her on her knees was enough to get me close to coming.

Still, much as I might've loved to hear her screaming my name while she came apart at the seams beneath my thrusts, I also wanted her first time to be something slightly more special than getting blasted from behind on some college jogging path. And, really, more than a good rut, what we both needed just then was for her to understand *exactly* the sort of relationship she was getting herself into.

So far, it seemed like she was on board with being my submissive. She certainly hadn't complained about that test swat I'd given her, which was both a huge relief and mildly hilarious considering that vampires were often just as aggressive as Dominant wolves were. (It was kind of hard not to be when your entire physiology had evolved around the concept of luring in prey through sexual seduction.) Even if she was an exception to the rule, though, Melody and I were still going to need to test the waters of her obedience just a little bit more before I was going to feel fully comfortable with taking the lead like I would if she were just another Beta or Omega in the pack.

Vampire or no, I refused to have a mate who didn't know her place.

And, god dammit, that's what she was, wasn't she? My mate. Mmph, just thinking about that phrase felt amazing.

She was mine.

And, hopefully, soon I would be hers.

This was all happening a lot faster than I'd ever thought it would back when I was growing up, but Mom had always said that when you knew, you knew. Plus, let's be real here, instinct had never steered me wrong before, so why would I start doubting it now?

"Right then," I declared, my mind made up and my libido kicking into overdrive. "Come here, you little brat."

Seizing a fistful of my mate's beautifully-dyed hair, I started dragging her toward the nearest stone bench I could see. It was high time she learned just what having such a cute ass was going to get her on the regular if we stayed together.

"Oh my gosh, Morgan! What are you doing?" she whined, voice cracking but otherwise not making any serious attempt to escape.

I chose to take that as a good sign, considering that she could have easily teleported away or snapped me in half like a twig if she wasn't enjoying what was happening to her.

"Use your powers of deduction, pet. I'm sure you can figure it out."

Plopping down onto the middle of the bench, I hauled her across my lap in one smooth, well-practiced motion.

Thank you, Sasha.

SMACK!

"Heeeey!"

Again, there came that adorable whining, this time

accompanied by a pair of high-tops kicking through the air beside me like they could somehow run away from what their owner had coming.

"Whaaaat?" I replied, mimicking Melody's exact cadence and drawing out a disgruntled harrumph from her in the process.

"That *hurt*."

"Uh-huh. Really?"

"Yes-"

SMACK!

"Really!"

"Why don't I believe you?"

SMACK!

"Because you're a big-"

SMACK!

"Meanie?"

"True, but that still doesn't change the fact that I'm not actually swatting you all that hard."

SMACK!

"Okay, fine, whatever, you're right," she admitted with a huff, revealing that her usually bright blue eyes had turned an iridescent shade of crimson as she threw a dirty look back at me like the brat she was. "But it still stung."

"Again, are you sure about that?"

SMACK!

"Yes, gosh dang it!"

SMACK!

"Seems to me like if it really did sting as much as you say, you'd be doing a lot more trying to escape right about now."

SMACK!

"After all, you don't *have* to take this spanking."

SMACK!

"We both know that you're fully capable of escaping any time you want to."

SMACK!

"Don't we, Melody?"

"I mean..."

SMACK!

"Ack! Okay, fine, I *might* like this... maybe just a little bit."

"Only a little bit?"

SMACK!

"Um, or maybe a lot a bit?" she wheedled in a tiny voice.

"Ah, so you *admit* you were lying just now?"

Realizing her mistake right about the same time that I bore my teeth at her in a triumphant grin, Melody's red eyes went wide with panic.

"Wait, I-!"

"Too late!"

SMACK!

"Owie!" she yelped, my much swifter swat producing a noticeable increase in her unintentionally lascivious hip wiggling.

SMACK!

"Okay, okay, that really does hurt!"

SMACK!

"Oh?"

SMACK!

"Does it?"

"Yes, gosh dang it!"

"Poor baby."

Pouting facetiously at my mate, I paused to rub the tautly-stretched seat of her jogging pants before swatting her just as hard again.

SMACK!

"Ack! Geez!" she squeaked, the preternaturally chilled muscles in her back tensing beneath where my hand had slipped under her shirt. "You know you don't have to try and impress me, right? I already like you."

"Awww, really?"

SMACK!

"Duh- Ack! Freaking shoot, owie!"

"Well, thank you, babe. That's good to know since I absolutely adore you."

SMACK!

"Urk!"

"Oh, and whine all you want, but we both know you can take a *lot* more than this."

SMACK!

"Can't you?"

SMACK!!

"*Can't you?*"

I put some serious *oomph* behind my swing that time. I'd already told her that I didn't like having to repeat myself, after all.

SMACK!!

"Ack! Yes, fine, I can!" she admitted in a garbled rush, her kicking picking up its pace as she changed tactics. "This still isn't fair, though!"

"So?"

"Soooo! Um-"

SMACK!!

"Owie!"

God, she was so compliant. Despite her whining, she still hadn't made any serious moves toward getting away.

"If you're going to-"

SMACK!!

"Frick-shoot! Spank me," she snapped through gritted teeth. "You have to at least give me a reason why!"

"Hmm..."

I got in a couple good squeezes, gauging just how thick and juicy my mate's ass truly was, under the guise of pretending to mull her argument over, before aiming a pair of hard swats at the backs of her thighs.

SMACK-SMACK!!

"No I don't."

"Yes you do!" Melody howled, furiously shaking her hips in a futile attempt to throw off some of that sting. "Mom always- Oh!"

Her hands flew up to cover her mouth with that partial revelation, and I cut loose with a cackle.

Guess that explains why she seems so at home over my knee.

"Awww, you are fucking adorable, you know that?"

I accompanied my cooing admiration with some light scratches between her shoulder blades that had her melting into a puddle across my lap.

"Sh-Shu-uh-ut up!"

"*Excuse me?*"

SMACK-SMACK!!

"Urk! I mean, shut up, please?"

"Better."

SMACK!!

"Hehe, thanks!" she snickered, hitting me with that same wild, feral grin that the other brats in my pack always seemed to adopt whenever it was time to put them in their place.

And here I was worrying she might not be into this.

"Okay, fine, you whiner. I suppose if you simply must have a reason why you're getting the spanking you've been all but begging for since the night we met we can say it's for you sucking my blood without permission before passing the fuck out in my bed all day."

"Um, I..."

Genuine worry tensed Melody's muscles at that, but I made short work of it with a reassuring rub up and down her spine, along with an accompanying squeeze to her sit-spots. With a shuddering sigh, she relaxed back into place, switching from panic to sass with the effortless ease of a born submissive no longer harboring a guilty conscience.

"That's not fair, though," she pouted, tossing her hair for good measure. "I can't help that I have to eat and sleep."

"So?"

SMACK!!

"So-"

SMACK!!

"Hey, come on! That actually does sting, you know!"

"Good."

SMACK!!

"It's supposed to."

Immediately, Melody's bravado collapsed back into fresh, albeit locally focused, distress as she tried to reach back and rub some of the sting out of where I'd just swatted her. I was more than ready for her, though.

"Oh no you don't!"

Intercepting her wrist, I pinned it against the small of her back and dished out three properly-punishing swats this time.

SMACK!! SMACK!! SMACK!!

"Ow! Oh! Owie!"

"You'll come to understand soon enough, my sweet Melody," I crooned, reveling in the sensation of her big bottom bouncing beneath my palm as I continued to rain down a merciless cascade of sizzling swats. "That I don't *need* to justify myself, to you or anyone else. I'm the pack Alpha here, which means that what I say goes. You got that?"

"What? But that's not-!"

SMACK!! SMACK!! SMACK!!

"I swear, if I hear you say 'that's not fair' one more fucking time..."

I finished that threat by yanking down her pants and panties, taking advantage of their stretchy waistbands to expose the roundest, jiggliest, most wonderfully full bubble butt I'd ever set eyes on in my entire life.

"Holy shit," I breathed, my mind screeching to a halt as her now bare cheeks broke out into goosebumps beneath the chilly caress of the late autumn air.

She really was perfect. Damn.

"M-Morgan, you can't just-!" Melody started to protest, her voice squeezing out of her panic-constricted throat a full octave higher than normal as she started to squirm. "Somebody might see!"

"Oh?" Perking up at that, I felt my face break out into a savage, hungry grin. "Now wouldn't that be just *terrible*?"

SMACK!! SMACK!! SMACK!!

The crack of my palm took on a much sharper report to it now as it bounced against my mate's bare skin, putting a stop to her pathetically adorable attempts to restore her shattered modesty. However, apparently still determined to keep fighting even in the face of overwhelming defeat, Melody started to jerk and pump her knees in time with my swats, trying (and failing spectacularly, I might add) to somehow work her hilariously juvenile and somehow very Mormon underwear back up her thighs.

"Oh, no, no, no, my precious little church girl. Those are staying right where they are."

"But… but…!"

Ignoring her protests while chuckling to myself, I leaned over and pushed her jogging pants and teddy bear panties all the way down to her fretfully scissoring ankles.

"Awww, don't tell me you're *embarrassed* by the idea of someone seeing you getting your bare-"

SMACK!!

"Bottom-"

SMACK!!

"Spanked?"

Melody didn't answer my question, so I decided to encourage her cooperation by twisting the knife just a bit more.

"Then again, I suppose if I'd let you keep your panties on, you'd still have a *bear* bottom, wouldn't you?"

That managed to wring a mortified groan out of the vampire, and another cackle from me.

The shy ones were always so much fun to break.

SMACK!! SMACK!! SMACK!!

Picking up the pace while continuing to put my back into each and every full-armed ***SMACK!!*** I watched with a widening grin as Melody's glorious globes wobbled and bounced, humming along as her musical voice sang out her displeasure with an ever-increasing plaintiveness that made me want to humiliate her all the more.

So I did.

How could I *not*?

"Just imagine it," I singsonged, licking my lips as I took my own advice. "They'd come around the bend, wondering what all the noise was about, and then-"

SMACK!!

"They'd get an eyeful of your fat-"

SMACK!!

"Juicy-"

SMACK!!

"Ass!"

SMACK!!

"Getting exactly what it deserves."

SMACK!! SMACK!! SMACK!!

"Yes they freaking would!" my mate agreed in a voice strangled with panicked arousal, making a valiant effort to reduce her exposure by clamping her thighs together.

"Uh-uh-uh, we can't be having that," I tutted, pausing her punishment to adjust her position atop my lap so that she was straddling my right leg with my knee wedging her thighs apart to further expose her clean-shaven pussy. "If our hypothetical witness is going to go through all the hypothetical trouble of making sure some very cute vampire freshman isn't getting murdered, they should at least be rewarded with a nice view for their trouble."

To help underscore just how on display she was now, I reached between Melody's splayed thighs and ran the pads of three fingers up and down her sopping folds.

"Ffff-ah!" she gasped, almost but not quite swearing as both feet and her head jerked up at the same time like she'd just been shocked. "A g-good deed should be its... oh gosh, its own reward!"

"A reward, huh?" Truth be told, I was genuinely impressed that she was able to come up with such a sassy rejoinder while sounding like she was on the verge of coming at any moment. "How about this then?"

Seizing a cheek in either hand, I spread them wide, revealing her puckered asshole to the moon above.

"Eep!"

"Mmmm, much better," I growled contentedly, giving each bun a couple of hard shakes before adjusting my grip so that only one hand was needed to keep her parted. "And, really, now that I think about it, you're totally right. Our would-be witness deserves to be given a proper demonstration of just how much of a horny little slut you are to compensate for you luring them all the way here under false pretenses."

Leaning over, I spat between Melody's cheeks, improvising some lube before using the middle finger on my free hand to tease at her anus.

"M-M-Morgan!" came her stuttering squeak of a reply.

"Yessss?" Keeping my tone oh so cruelly casual, I circled the rim of her nervous little pucker over and over again before wriggling the tip of my finger inside of her, pushing out a breathy gasp of mingled humiliation and delight from her in the process. "Use your words now, pet."

"Words, words, words!"

"Heh. A for effort. Guess that means you're ready for some of this."

"Ah! Ah! Oh my gosh!"

You know, for someone who was a total anal virgin, I couldn't help but notice that Melody was handling my finger surprisingly well. Offering only token resistance as I experimentally pushed inside of her all the way up to my knuckles.

Well now, that certainly opens up some interesting opportunities, I mused while idly pumping in and out of her with first one finger and then two. She was whimpering in discomfort in between throaty little gasps, but I had a sneaking suspicion she could probably handle three fingers without much trouble. *Or maybe even my…*

Ahem. But I was getting distracted, wasn't I?

"Okay, enough playing around," I declared with a put-upon sigh, withdrawing my fingers from inside my mate and returning my left hand to the small of her back. "We still have a spanking to take care of."

Shaking my head at Melody's wantonly disappointed groan as her cheeks wobbled back into place, I once again set about lighting her bare bottom on fire.

SMACK!! SMACK!! SMACK!!

"Ack! Frick! Shoot, shoot, shoot!"

Despite her distressed gyrations and pained cries to the contrary, Melody's body was telling me an entirely different story as I continued to dish out a truly ruthless spanking. Without anything to stem the tide, the insides of her thighs (along with most of my knee) had become drenched in arousal, sped along by her hips bucking and writhing against my thigh in a transparent attempt to find enough friction to come.

Oops, can't have that, I thought to myself with a smirk, circling an arm around her waist and hoisting her up just enough to put my leg out of range of her clit as I continued to blister her backside.

SMACK!! SMACK!! SMACK!!

By far the most fascinating thing about spanking my very vocal vampire on her very bare bottom was, well, her bottom.

Aside from the wonderful jiggle my swats were able to produce now that there wasn't anything there to get in the way, I could see too that her cheeks were also doing some rather interesting things.

SMACK!! SMACK!! SMACK!!

"Shoot! Dang! Ow! Okay, that one was way too- Oh! Mean!"

With each thunderous impact of my palm (Which was really starting to sting. This was why paddles were a thing, dammit!), her cheeks would compress and then spring back with a mesmerizing ripple as the white handprint I'd left behind flooded with pink. Only, instead of staying there and gradually blending in with the others that had come before until her entire bottom was a uniform shade of bright, burning red, said handprint started to fade almost as soon as it had appeared, leaving me with a fresh canvas by the time my next swat found its mark.

Well, shit.

Seeing this advanced bit of vampire healing in action, I shed the last few remaining vestiges of my (admittedly, not actually all that abundant) restraint. Clearly, Melody could take the sort of spanking I'd only ever dreamed of giving, and I found myself going absolutely buck-fucking-wild on her adorable ass as a result.

SMACK-SMACK-SMACK-SMACK!!!

"Morgan, I-! Owie, owie, owie!"

Even if I couldn't build up a sustained inferno like I wanted to, she was definitely still feeling every furiously burning bit of my full-armed swats as they meteored into her, which was a decent compromise. I wanted her to at least have *something* sore to sit on once we were done here, even if that lingering ache was confined entirely to her imagination.

"Okay, okay, that's enough!" Melody yelped after another minute of solid, nonstop spanking. "I've learned my lesson or whatever."

"Doubt it, little miss smartass."

"I have!" she insisted with a high-pitched squeal as I turned my attention to the backs of those pale, creamy thighs.

"Yeah, well, maybe once this ass is starting to smart properly, I'll be convinced."

"Now who's- Ack! Being a smart- Owie! Butt?"

Okay, I'll admit it. That one got me.

And I, in turn, got her.

SMACK-SMACK-SMACK-SMACK!!!

All up and down her dancing thighs while we both laughed out loud at her knee-jerk deference to Jesus-approved profanity.

"I'm serious!" she eventually managed, her giggles having turned somewhat hysterical while I'd continued to absolutely blister her buns. "I promise I'll be good."

"Oh, I know you will," I said with a shrug, my grin so big now that it was starting to hurt my cheeks. (Though nowhere near as much as I was hurting hers.) "I'm still not stopping, though."

"But-!"

SMACK-SMACK-SMACK-SMACK!!!

"The only 'but' I care about right now is this one," I cut her off by saying, borrowing one of my mom's reliable standbys for uncooperative brats as I dished out a lightning-fast series of swats to the meatiest parts of Melody's bouncing buns.

SMACK-SMACK-SMACK-SMACK!!!

"Oh my gosh, you are such a- Fuh-rick! Meanie!"

Despite being said with a laugh, it seemed to have finally dawned on her that she was stuck there until *I* decided she'd had enough, not the other way around, and with that revelation came a marked (and oh so welcome) increase in her writhing across my lap. Had I been a regular human attempting to spank her girlfriend, her spirited squirming would have definitely posed an issue, but we wolves weren't without our own touch of supernatural strength. Granted, mine was nowhere near as much as what Melody could bring to bear were she truly pissed off, but she still seemed to have come to accept that she wasn't going anywhere until I was through with her. And, judging by the way her yelping and cries had taken on a distinctly *moaning* quality to them, she wasn't nearly as upset about her situation as she was leading me to believe.

SMACK-SMACK-SMACK-SMACK!!!

Watching my new mate (damn, that still felt so wild to think about and I loved it!) go through her first real taste of total submission was downright beautiful and I knew it would be playing in my mind over and over again for the next few days any time I felt so much as a twinge of arousal.

First, she started to panic as we at last found her pain tolerance threshold and I breezed right past it without slowing down in the slightest. Then, came bristling indignation as she fought to maintain some semblance of control over the situation.

"You can't do this to me!"

SMACK-SMACK-SMACK-SMACK!!!

"This isn't funny!"

SMACK-SMACK-SMACK-SMACK!!!

And so on.

Next came bargaining.

"I'll be good! I'll be good!"

SMACK-SMACK-SMACK-SMACK!!!

"Whatever you want! I promise I'll do whatever you want!"

SMACK-SMACK-SMACK-SMACK!!!

Then, sweetest of all, came surrender. Total and complete, brimming with trust and a heartfelt desire to serve, as something intangible but unmistakable snapped into place around our souls, linking us inextricably together forever.

She was mine, and I was hers.

Now and always.

"Breathe it out, baby. We're almost done."

Wordlessly, Melody obeyed, and I rewarded her for her efforts by absolutely obliterating her sit-spots. Pouring all of my rapidly-dwindling strength into pounding out an explosive tattoo right where her rippling cheeks met her dancing thighs.

SMACK-SMACK-SMACK-SMACK!!!

Her kicking became truly frantic then, further exposing her drenched pussy along with little peeks of her puckered anus more and more frequently, and it was taking all of my self-control not to go after them. Again, though, I reminded myself that her first time deserved to be special. (Shut up, that light ass fucking earlier doesn't count!) So, instead of sinking my fingers into as many holes as I could at once, I contended myself with memorizing every dip and curve of her writhing body as I did my best to make sure she'd be thinking of me every time she sat down tomorrow.

Or, well, maybe more like the next five minutes.

Much as I was doing everything I could to deliver a world-class hiding, she was still a vampire. Which meant that even while kicking and complaining over my knee, she still recovered fast enough that it was a perpetual (and often losing) uphill battle to outpace her healing abilities enough for some proper burning to settle in.

SMACK-SMACK-SMACK-SMACK!!!

Ugh. I'd definitely need to come up with something better in the long run if I was ever going to have any hope of making a proper impression on her when it inevitably came time to truly discipline her. Melody was soft and kind and painfully earnest, which meant that as her Dominant it would be my responsibility to help her rise above her self-doubt and bad habits so that she could reach the full potential we both knew she was capable of. That was a problem for another night, though. For now, all I needed to focus on was finishing off my naughty girl before sending her on her way.

Ah, the joys of catch and release.

SMACK-SMACK-SMACK-SMACK!!!

After a dozen more full-armed, full-strength swats to Melody's sit-spots, I started to gradually ease up. Continuing to pepper her generous seat with lighter and lighter spanks until, finally, I came to a stop with my hand resting atop the center of her once again perfectly pale bare bottom.

Fuck, my arm was killing me. Something that soft and squishy had no right being that tough.

"Right. I think that... ought to… ought to keep you on your toes for a little while," I panted, noting with some chagrin that I was the only one out of breath between the two of us as I grabbed Melody by the hair again and dragged her up off of my leg.

"Oh!" she gasped, more startled than in pain it would seem as she swam through an ocean of adrenaline, endorphins, and no doubt some specialized vampire hormones that had her feeling pretty damn good if the dreamy expression on her face was anything to go by.

She'd kicked off her pants and underwear at some point in the last few minutes, leaving her completely naked below the waist. A fact which I took immediate advantage of by forcing her back down onto my lap, straddling my left leg this time while she faced me.

"Um, hey," she ventured tentatively, smiling shyly up at me through her thoroughly messed up bangs.

"Hey yourself, sweet thing."

Her face was close enough that I could count each and every one of her thick black eyelashes. And, *mmph*, she was just as wet as I was. It was enough to drive a woman to distraction!

Slightly more concerning (and also extremely hot, not going to lie), however, was the fact that her half-lidded pupils were still glowing a very distinct shade of vampiric crimson. And, much as I would have loved to have gotten lost in those beautiful baby, er… reds while their owner stared up at me from between my legs, the fact that said owner was also eyeballing my neck like it owed her money gave me pause. Clearly, she'd managed to find her appetite again somewhere between when I'd yanked her over my knee and now, and while a nonstop cascade of orgasms was certainly tempting, I really wasn't in the mood to carry a blood-drunk freshman all the way back home again.

I guess I could try slinging her over the back of my bike?

Maybe tie her down with some bungees? Hmm... Nah, better not risk it. That would be one awkward ticket for sure. Oh well, Plan B it is then!

With my mind made up, I wrenched Melody's head back by my hold on her hair and crushed my lips to hers, making her squeal as I claimed her mouth with the sort of savage, animal fury that my libido grudgingly accepted as a consolation prize. It was no oral, but it would do.

The scents of cupcakes, copper, and lots and lots of lust swamped my senses as we sat there making out for what felt like forever, my free hand pawing mercilessly at her ass while I slanted my mouth against hers to push my tongue in past those all-too-willing lips. There, I toyed with the tips of her fangs just to hear her whimper, knowing full well that I was seriously tempting fate if I nicked myself in the process, before wrestling her tongue into submission as she ground against my thigh with reckless abandon, soaking through the dark denim of my jeans yet again.

I was definitely going to have to change when I got home, and I couldn't have cared less. Not when I had her scent all over me.

"Come for me," I commanded in a brusque murmur, pulling back to catch my breath as we locked eyes again. "Let me hear you sing, my sweet Melody."

"Y-Yes, ma'am!"

Ever the dutiful submissive, Melody did exactly as she was told, arching her back and rolling her hips against my rhythmically bouncing thigh while she howled my name to the moon above.

Heh. So much for not wanting to draw any attention.

Not that I particularly cared, mind you. Frankly, I was way too proud of how loud I was able to make my submissive scream to really give a shit about anybody seeing her doing it. And, besides, Melody was putting on the sort of show that practically demanded an audience.

Because, like, *damn.*

Whether it was a consequence of her vampiric biology, or just natural good luck, it turned out that my mate was one of those girls who could jump from one orgasm to the next with only a brief pause in between. A talent which she demonstrated for me over, and over, and *over* again as I dug my nails into her bare hips and helped grind her pussy into my leg. Until, eventually, I was pretty sure I'd managed to wring every last climax out of her that I was likely to get before she passed out from pure sensory overload.

"There we go. I've got you, baby. Just breathe it out..."

Rubbing steadying circles against the small of Melody's back while she panted into the crook of my neck (her eyes having returned to their original icy blue, I was pleased to see), I waited until I was reasonably sure that she wasn't going to collapse into a puddle of boneless, post-orgasm goop before easing her gently off of my lap and standing up after her.

Then, because it was just too good of an opportunity to pass up, I bent down and scooped up her discarded joggers and panties before she remembered she wasn't wearing them.

"I'll see you later," I said with an extremely self-satisfied smirk, fishing her phone from out of her pocket and turning her hand up to set it onto her palm, folding her fingers over it to keep her from accidentally dropping it.

Finally snapping out of her trance, Melody stirred to attention with an indignant squeak that had me seriously reconsidering putting her back across my lap, thoroughly sore shoulder be damned.

"Wait, you're *leaving*?"

"Mmhmm, I've got a thesis to work on and I'm sure you've got homework too," I said, doing my best to keep it cool.

Much as I would've loved to take her home with me, I knew that she needed time to herself to cool off and think things through before we took our relationship any further.

"I mean..." Melody hesitated, fresh color warming her cheeks.

"Uh-huh. Thought so." Leaning in, I planted a quick kiss on her ruby lips. "Get home safe, yeah?"

Before turning and heading off back the way we'd come with a spring in my step.

Which was right about the time it clicked for Melody that I still had her pants and underwear.

"Heyyyy!" Her whine echoed around the small clearing as she materialized in front of me with a stomp. "Give those back!"

"Hmmm, nope, don't think I will," I replied with a shit-eating grin, sidestepping past her and continuing on my way.

Rather than teleport in front of me again and force the issue, Melody instead let out an exasperated growl that very nearly had me breaking out in laughter with how impotently adorable it was.

"Oh my gosh, you are such a freaking meanie, you know that? What the heck am I supposed to do without pants? I'm *naked*, for crying out loud!"

"You've still got your shirt on, don't you?"

"That's not what I mean and you know it!" she snapped, tugging down on the front of said shirt in an attempt to cover her groin and inadvertently further exposing her bare ass in the process.

Okay, this time I did laugh.

"You're a smart girl," I teased, salivating at the sight of that clean-shaven pussy peeking out from between her firmly pressed together thighs. "I'm sure you'll figure something out."

"But... but...!"

I'm pretty sure it took Melody a lot longer than she would have liked to admit for her orgasm-addled brain to remember that she was fully capable of teleporting her vampire butt back home without being seen by anybody.

"Oh. Uh. Right."

"I put my number in your phone. Shoot me a text later, yeah?" I told her, blowing her a kiss. "I had a lot of fun tonight and I want to see you again soon."

Tension bled from Melody's bunched up shoulders then. Like she'd somehow still been afraid I didn't like her or something after everything we'd just done. Poor girl. We'd definitely need to work on those self-esteem issues at some point. In the meantime, though, I was very much looking forward to her fulfilling her next test of obedience for me.

Even if it *was* just reaching out to say hello.

"Ciao, sweet cheeks. I'll see you later."

And, with that, I was gone. Loping off in search of something to eat and one of my more submissive pack mates to take care of some of my other pent up needs.

Operation Track Down Melody and Spank Her Silly had been a complete success.

CHAPTER 6

Morgan

Loping along at a steady pace, my shoes crunching at regular intervals against the dead leaves and loose gravel underfoot, I could see now why Melody favored these paths around campus so much for hunting. Lots of overgrowth to obscure sight lines while stalking prey *and* plenty of scrub to pull a kill into? Hell, if we were into chasing down humans, the girls and I would be all over this place. Still, none of that was the reason why I'd chosen this particular place for my evening run. No, the reason for that was something a lot simpler.

Three days! Three fucking days!

Cutting loose with the sort of low, rumbling growl that sent every small animal within a half-mile radius scrambling for cover, I gritted my teeth and started tearing across the trail as fast as I could without actually letting my inner wolf rise to the surface. Kicking up big sprays of dirt and gravel in my wake.

Look, don't get me wrong, I understood that this was new territory for Melody and that the responsible thing to do was to stand back and give her enough space to make the next move when she felt comfortable doing so, but come the fuck on. There was being patient, and then there was letting your submissive chicken out on you over and over again because she was raised by a bunch of religious fundamentalists who beat it into her head that wanting to kiss girls would send you straight to hell.

"Fucking shit-ass magic underwear wearing motherfuckers!"

The only thing that was keeping me from totally losing it and going over to her apartment to force the issue, was the fact that whenever I checked the text conversation I'd started with her so that I could save my number into her phone (about once every hour, but that's neither here nor there, so shut up), I would occasionally see those three blinking dots that meant that she was typing something. Whatever it was she wrote, though, she never actually sent it, and I was seriously starting to worry that she might never talk to me again at this rate.

I mean, damn. It wasn't like I was going to bite her or anything.

Well, okay, yes, I *was* planning on biting her (and spanking her, and fucking her, and probably doing a whole bunch of other things I couldn't think of off the top of my head), but it wasn't like she wasn't going to enjoy it! We both knew what she was into.

I had the cum stains on my favorite pair of jeans to prove it.

Fuck it. If I don't hear from her by sunrise, I'm taking matters into my own hands, mating protocol be damned.

It's not like we hadn't already jumped the gun on most of that stuff anyway. And, really, now that I thought about it, she *had* been raised human, hadn't she? It would stand to reason then that if I was going to get the gears turning here, I'd need to do something besides pinning her down and biting her neck until she was ready to submit.

Hmmm... Yeah, a little touch of romance ought to be just the thing to get her butt into gear.

With the beginnings of a plan starting to coalesce in the back of my head, I was starting to feel like I could actually breathe again, and it occurred to me that I should probably slow down to something approaching a more reasonable pace for an athletic grad student just in case I ran into anybody out here who wasn't a bratty vampire in need of an ass blistering and a whole bunch of kisses.

I was just hitting a comfortable stride, when my phone started going off.

"Ugh, what now?"

For a brief moment, my chest tightened with the hope that it might be Melody, but a quick check of the display confirmed that it wasn't. And, while normally I'd have just sent the call straight to voicemail so I could finish my run in peace, when the reigning Alpha of the entire Bloodfang pack decides to give you a call, you pick up.

"Hi, Mom," I panted, jogging to a stop and stepping off the path to lean against a tree.

"Hey there, sweet pea."

Oh god, I could straight up hear how smug she was from here.

Fuck.

"Okay, who told you?"

My mother's answering cackle was all the confirmation I needed to know I was well and truly busted.

"Dani. Who else?"

"Why that chatty little bitch. I swear I'm-"

"Now, you quit that growling right this second, missy. She did exactly what she was supposed to," my mother scolded, actually waiting for me to take in and blow out a couple of deep, calming breaths before she continued. "So, who's the lucky lady? It *is* a lady isn't it?"

"Of course it is!"

"All right, all right, I was just checking."

More like teasing, given the way she was still laughing.

"Were all those times you walked in on me and Margo back when I was a teenager not enough?" I deadpanned with the sort of eye roll I'd never have been able to get away with back when I actually was a teenager.

"Stop trying to avoid the question, Morgan Anne."

"Oooh, middle name, real scary, *Mom*. Does that shit actually work on Kate?"

"Like you wouldn't believe."

Any semblance of parental authority my mother might have still held over me dissolved then as we shared a laugh over her extremely submissive partner's inability to fight back against her middle name being weaponized against her. And, just like that, we were back to our usual dynamic of equally-dominant Alphas.

"You two are adorable, you know that?"

"Yes. Yes we are. Now, spill it, child, before your mama and I decide to come down there and sniff this girl out for ourselves."

"Don't you fucking dare!"

"Morgan..."

"Fine, fine." Scrubbing a hand through my sweaty hair, I paused to shake my head before saying with a smirk, "Her name's Melody, she's a freshman, and I plucked her up at a leather bar a little over a week ago. There. Happy now?"

"A leather bar? Seriously? Huh. I'd always pictured you as the top."

My mom, ladies and gentlemen, ever the comedian.

"Fuck off, you know damn well who's fucking who," I snapped, not bothering to hide the savage pride in my voice as memories of Melody breathlessly grinding against my thigh sprang to the forefront of my mind's eye. "Her virgin ass was toast the second I got my hands on it."

"Wait, a *virgin*? I thought you said you met her at a leather bar?"

"I did. Apparently, she figured the best way to come out of the closet was by jumping straight into the deep end."

"Head first, by the sound of it. Jesus. It's a miracle she didn't wind up fucked and dumped without her wallet behind some dumpster. Your mama and I have been to bars like that before, and not everyone knows how to take no for an answer."

"Tell me about it. I spent half the night serving up death

glares," I growled, remembering the gravitational pull for handsy butches my mate's perfectly-sculpted ass seemed to have developed the moment we hit the dance floor. "On the bright side, I'm pretty sure she could hold her own in a fight if push came to shove."

"What? Is she secretly a kung fu holy sister or something?"

It was my turn to snort this time.

"Heh. Funny you should mention karate nuns, but, no. I'm pretty sure the only black belts that girl has are the ones she's shoplifted from Hot Topic."

"Mmmm, a good girl gone bad with just a hint of danger? Sounds yummy."

"Try ex-Mormon and leaning real hard into a newfound goth aesthetic. But you're definitely right about her being tasty. I wound up marking her the night we met."

"Excuse me, what?! MORGAN!"

"You heard me." Buffing my nails against my shirt, I felt myself swelling with pride. "Honestly, part of me is still a little shocked by how sudden it all was. One second I'm holding her at knifepoint while choking her out, and the next I'm claiming her while she's coming buckets under me. But, hey, the bite took, and when you know, you know, right?"

"That's more or less how it was for me and your mama, yep. Though, in our case it was nylon rope and some nipple clamps," Mom agreed, getting over her initial shock surprisingly quick before turning deadly serious. "And you have exactly three seconds to send me pictures, young lady."

"Uh-huh. Whatever."

Rolling my eyes, but unable to stop myself from grinning like an idiot, I put my mom on speaker and proceeded to send her a handful of the selfies Melody and I had taken that night at the Jackalope.

"Morgan!" Came her excited shouting as soon as my message had sent. "She. Is. *Precious!*"

"Damn right she is."

Mom's tone turned sly then.

"So, is it true what they say about those goody two shoes church girls?"

"That they come the second you drop a digit on them?" I finished for her, as we both shared a snicker. "It sure fucking is. Plus, she's also got a submissive streak a mile wide and an ass that just won't quit."

"I can see that," Mom agreed, before breaking down in a distinctly un-Alpha-like fit of cooing. "Awww, look at the two of you smiling together! She seems perfect for you, honey. Does she make you happy?"

"She really does," I sighed contentedly. Then, because there really was no smooth way of bringing it up, I pinched the bridge of my nose and added in a rush, "Also, she's a vampire."

"She's WHAT?!"

If my mom kept screaming like that, she was going to blow out the speaker on my phone.

"What, are you going deaf?" I snapped, relieved that she was yelling and not turning all soft and serious. "That's why I had her at knifepoint in the first place. She bit me out of nowhere when we were about to head home, and I wasn't sure if she was an assassin or not. She's not, by the way in case you're wondering, I was apparently just too hot for her to ignore is all."

Mom didn't even pretend to laugh at that last bit.

"Does she know you're a wolf?"

"Of course she does!"

"And her seethe isn't shitting its collective leather pants at you snapping up one of their own?"

"Uh... Yeah. Funny thing, that," I hesitated, not used to being at a loss for words. "She, uh... She doesn't have one."

"Excuse me?"

Ah, *there* was that deadly calm I'd been waiting for.

"Look. She says she was only turned a few months ago, and that she has no idea who her sire is. They apparently bailed before she came to, all right?"

"Seriously?"

"Yep."

I could practically hear Mom massaging her temples in tandem with me as we each blew out a frustrated breath.

"Well now, *that* could be an issue."

"What?" My heart skipped a beat at that, and not in the fun way. "Why?"

"Because the North American Sanguinary Council takes their population policies very fucking seriously."

"Oh."

"'Oh' is right, kiddo. This is some 'stake you to the ground, cut out your heart, and let the sun do its thing' ritual execution stuff we're talking about here. If they find out they've got an unauthorized Risen running around, it's going to get real ugly real fast for your church girl."

Hearing that, my teeth sharpened to points and a shimmer of dark brown pelt rippled across my arms. I was one breath away from going full on fairy tale nightmare monster, potential witnesses be damned.

"Nobody is touching my mate," I snarled, squeezing my phone so hard it was a miracle it didn't crack.

"Easy now, hon, *easy*. We're not to that stage yet," Mom soothed. "I'll reach out to my contacts on the council and see if we can't discreetly get the ball rolling on finding her sire so we can make her nice and legal. There'll be some bureaucratic headaches and probably some saber rattling before this is all said and done, but It'll be fine, I'm sure. Just sit tight and keep her out of trouble until we get this sorted, all right?"

"That was the plan, yeah." I gritted. "If I have my way, she'll be moving into the house come Monday."

"Good."

We were both silent for nearly a full minute after that, each of us caught up in our own swirling thoughts, before Mom finally spoke again.

"She's really the one for you, isn't she?"

"She really is," I sighed, my heart still pounding the ever-loving shit out of chest despite my best efforts to get it to calm the fuck down. "I might've bitten her on impulse, but I can't get her out of my head, and I'm pretty sure she's in the same boat."

"Oh, baby, I'm so proud of you!"

Mom had swung back into maximum motherly exuberance mode now, and she covered her receiver to shout to my other mom. It was muffled, but I still managed to pick up something about good news and her owing her twenty bucks.

Sure enough, there came Mama Kate's distant holler just a second later.

"Congrats, Morgan!" she shouted, no doubt from her studio on the other side of the cabin she and Mom shared. "Bring her home for Thanksgiving!"

"Planning on it!" I yelled back, more because I was starting to overflow with excitement of my own than because I thought it might make me easier to hear.

God, I missed them.

"All right, baby, I'll take care of the council stuff for you," Mom said then. "You two just worry about working on that mate bond. Kate and I want grandbabies, you hear?"

"Um, is that even possible with her being what she is?"

"What? Don't be silly, of course it is! She's a vampire, she's not barren."

"Uh… You sure about that?"

"Morgan, honey, she has special dietary needs and *maybe* a pact with the forces of darkness that linger on the periphery of our reality. Her womb, on the other hand, is just fine and you'd hardly be the first wolf and vampire bonded pair to produce pups."

"Wait, really?"

"Do you remember your cousin Michelle?"

"Yeah…"

"Her father's a vampire. He's the council's overseas liaison for Europe, actually. They met while her mother was on vacation in

Italy and were mated less than a week later. So, don't go tying yourself into knots over how fast this is happening or whether or not you'll be able to breed her. You're a perfectly healthy Dominant, and from what you've told me, she sounds like an ideal submissive."

"Oh. Well, uh, guess that's good to know," I allowed, my face flushing with warmth at the thought of impregnating Melody. I had no idea if that was something she'd even want, but it was nice to know that we at least had the *option*. Not going to lie, being unable to produce an heir for the pack had had me more than a little worried these last few days. "But, yeah, I wouldn't go holding my breath on the baby front if I were you. I'm way more interested in fucking her ass than I am in knocking it up right now."

"Awww, my baby the romantic."

"Like mother, like daughter."

"Damn straight," agreed Mom with a laugh. "All right, tell your mate we say hi, and you be sure to call your mama later, she misses you!"

"I will, I will," I promised, fighting down a laugh of my own at the indignant squawk of agreement Mom's reprimand produced from Kate. "Talk to you later. I love you both."

"Us too, sweetheart."

CHAPTER 7

Melody

A few nights after my humiliating (and way too much fun) run in with Morgan and her friends / pack / girl gang, I woke up to find a huge glass vase overflowing with the most beautiful blood red roses and crimson carnations I'd ever seen perched precariously atop my apartment's rickety as heck kitchen table.

"Dang. Who decided to bankrupt a flower shop?" I asked my roommate, Chloe, as she sat down beside the miniature botanical garden to pull on her boots before heading out for her graveyard shift at the grocery story I liked to shoplift Momo's food from.

"You tell me," she said with such a look of conspiratorial pride on her face that I instantly felt color starting to creep its way up my neck.

"Wait. They're for *me*?"

"Sure are!"

"Wha-? I- That's... Huh."

Chloe's excitement only intensified as I turned back to regard the explosion of color that my cat was currently trying to decide if she could eat or not.

"Just, 'huh'?" Chloe pressed, carefully batting away Momo before she could make herself sick.

"Nobody's ever gotten me flowers before," I admitted, my lips quirking up at the corners.

"Jesus. Seriously? Not even for prom?"

"Are you kidding me? Like my parents would ever let me go to prom with a girl."

"Ah, yeah. Fair point." Chloe's mouth twisted into a disapproving pucker at my upbringing before just as quickly snapping back into a broad grin. "Well, fuck them. You've got flowers now, and the lady who dropped them off was fine as hell."

"Lady? What lady?"

Okay, okay, I had *one* idea who it might be, but I didn't want to get my hopes up. Not after I'd been ghosting her like a freaking coward these last few days.

"Oh yeah," my roommate nodded, oblivious to my internal conflict as she stood up and gestured with a hand above her head. "About this tall, crazy cute side shave, and abs for days?"

"Oh my gosh!" I squealed, fully rounding on Chloe now as a burst of giddy adrenaline eclipsed my anxiety. "Did she say her name was Morgan?"

"Morgan!" Chloe clapped a hand to her forehead. "That's what it was. I kept thinking Marsha for some reason."

"Oh my gosh, oh my gosh, oh my gosh!"

My kinda-sorta-maybe girlfriend didn't hate me after all. Instead, she'd brought me flowers!

Taking my roommate by the hands, I danced us around the living room, sending Momo skittering for cover on top of the refrigerator in the process.

"She likes me. She likes me. She really, really likes me!"

I mean, I'd had a suspicion she might, but it was still nice to have it confirmed.

As soon as that thought hit me, though, I was punched in the gut by another burst of self-doubt.

"Wait. Oh crap. People don't send flowers for break ups, do they?"

There wasn't a card with the flowers as far as I could see, but that didn't mean Morgan hadn't given Chloe a message for me.

"Huh? No, of course they don't," she answered, freeing her hands before I could spin us around the coffee table for a third time as she tilted her head at me in confusion. "Maybe a text if they're really shitty, but she seemed way into you when she was here."

She waved an arm toward my flowers then.

"You don't go dropping the kind of cash it takes for an arrangement like *that* on someone you don't want to see anymore. That's easily a hundred dollars' worth of flowers, and that's before you take into account the vase."

"I…" That had my face flushing an even brighter shade of pink and my stomach shriveling into a lead ball as I flopped down onto our threadbare couch with a miserable groan, burying my face in my hands. "Craaaap! What the heck am I supposed to do now? She told me text her a few days ago, and I still haven't done it."

"What? Why not? It's just a text."

"Well, *yeah*, but it's not, like, *just* a text, is it?" I exploded, propelled back to my feet by a surge of mortified indignation. "She said she wanted *me* to text *her*, and I haven't! She hasn't called me either, and I want to text her, really I do, but I can't just hit her with a 'hi' and call it quits, now can I? So, I've been *trying* to think of something fun and witty to send her, but every time I think I've got something, I chicken out at the last second and delete it, and now it's Monday and I-!"

"Whoa now!" my roommate interjected before I could burst into the tears that were threatening to break free at any moment. "Deep breaths, hon."

"But!"

"Shush."

To my surprise, Chloe pressed a pair of fingertips to my lips, holding them there until she was certain I was going to remain silent.

"Look. Obviously this girl is into you," she continued. "Like I said, you don't go out of your way to hand deliver a metric fuck-ton of flowers to someone you don't like. Now, you're going to stop having a meltdown, and then you're going to go bring me your phone. Okay?"

"Um, okay?"

Maybe I'd been spending too much time around bossy were-wolves, or maybe I was just starting to realize I was someone who naturally did better being told what to do. Whatever the case may be, the next thing I knew, I was unlocking my phone and handing it off to my roommate.

"Do you trust me?" she asked, meeting my eye with a serious expression.

I took a moment to mull that over, before nodding yes, my face still burning. We'd been assigned to each other by random lottery from the university's housing department, but Chloe and I had become fast friends almost immediately. Like Morgan, she was just too hard not to like.

"Good."

With that one word, Chloe marched right up to our table, took a picture of the arrangement Morgan had sent me, typed something out on my messenger, and hit send.

"There. Problem solved," she said with an exasperated roll of her eyes, tossing my phone back to me (which I fumbled twice before managing to actually catch) and moving to pull on her coat.

"What did you-?" I started to ask, before remembering that I could just look at my phone and see for myself. "Oh my gosh, *Chloe*!"

"Sorry- Kssh! Can't hear you!" my roommate called over her shoulder, making pretend static noises as she hurried out of our apartment. "Bye, Mel, have fun with your girlfriend!"

"Ugh! You are such a-!"

But, the front door had already slammed shut, and I was suddenly left alone in our living room to deal with the fallout of my roommate's "help."

"Well, frick."

Looking down at my phone again, I felt my stomach twist itself into knots.

[Totes luv these! U r def getting laid tonight. ;)]

"I can't believe she-!"

Before I could give voice to my (extremely) conflicted feelings on my roommate's choice in opening lines, I just about had a heart attack as I watched those three blinking dots appear on the left side of my screen, before being replaced by a response from Morgan.

[You're damn right I am.]

[OMG that was my roommate!] I hurriedly typed, all the while failing spectacularly not to think about what having sex with Morgan might feel like.

[LOL I was wondering where that came from.]

[Hey! I can be bold when I want to!]

[Sure you can.]

[I CAN! >:( ]

[Care to prove that?]

Oh gosh, I could just picture her pointy and kind of scary grin along with the way her amber eyes would be stirring toward gold as I read that, and before I could stop myself, I typed back, *[You're on.]*

Morgan left me hanging for a full two and a half minutes then (I counted), before her next message finally came through.

[All right, fine. Send nudes.]

[Ass, titties, V, everything.]

[I want to see what you've been hiding from me these last few days, pet.]

I nearly dropped my phone again as I read and reread that, before two more messages came through.

[Or don't.]

[Seriously. I'm fine going at whatever pace you're comfortable with. I just want to be with you. <3]

"Oh gosh, that's..."

Heat and something else, something that had always been there but had only made itself known these last couple weeks, unspooled inside my chest then as it finally hit me.

I *wanted* this.

I wanted Morgan to tell me what to do, and to grab my butt, and to call me embarrassing nicknames. Heck, I even wanted to send her naked pictures!

More than any of that, though. What I wanted most of all was simply to be...

Wanted.

All this time, even before I'd become a vampire, I'd been hoping and praying (back when I still prayed, at least) that someone would eventually come along who would love me for me, instead of a me that conformed to some checklist of what I was "supposed" to be. Ever since that afternoon at Wendy's when I was twelve, pretending to eat french fries while my dad yelled at me because he'd found porn on the family computer (*lesbian* porn, no less!) and I'd realized that he and Mom would never accept me because I was fundamentally flawed in their bigoted eyes, I think I'd pulled inside myself. Content to fly under the radar and do whatever I was supposed to so long as it meant I wouldn't get hurt or judged.

That shell had started to crack after I'd been turned, but then Morgan had blown through and completely shattered it in a single night.

She made me feel wanted.

She made me feel special.

She made me feel like there was actually something worth loving inside myself, and all I wanted was to be by her side. Forever and always.

Okay, wow, girl, you've got it bad.

I did, and I didn't care that we'd just met. Or that she was way more experienced with all this stuff than I was. She'd gotten under my skin and into my heart, and I'd never been happier.

Which was kind of ironic, since by all rights I *should* be furious with her for what she'd done to me on the trail the other night. But, I just... wasn't. In fact, I think I wanted her to do it again. (Although, mayyyybe not as hard as she had toward the end there.) Either way, there was no denying how much I'd loved being over Morgan's lap while she forced me submit to her. Stranger still, even though she'd been so rough with me, so commanding and domineering, I'd genuinely never felt safer. She was just so strong and in control, and I understood on a fundamental level that she would never let anything bad happen to me.

That she loved me.

That I was hers.

So, stripping off my pajamas right there in the middle of the living room, I went sprinting for the bathroom I shared with Chloe. (Forgetting for the moment that I could just teleport.) There, with the door securely locked behind me, just in case my roommate came back unexpectedly, I proceeded to take what was probably way too many mirror selfies from just about every angle I could think of (thank goodness that whole no reflection stereotype wasn't actually a thing), before sending my favorites to Morgan before I could stop to second guess myself.

I wanted this.

I *needed* this.

[Awww, look at you!]

[Church girls make for the most adorable sluts. >:)]

Blushing to the roots of my hair and very deliberately not focusing on how amazing my boobs looked in the last picture I'd sent her, I replied back with a series of praying hands emojis, followed by a few peaches for good measure.

[Okay, yeah. You are so getting it next time I see you, you little brat.]

And there went my heart again.

What kind of "it" were we talking about here? Was she going to spank me? Or maybe…

[Tonight?]

Holy crap, who was this bold new Melody who sent nudes to her girlfriend and made the first move on setting up a date?

[Sounds great.]

This time, a picture accompanied Morgan's response. It was a selfie of her flexing in front of her own bathroom mirror while looking absurdly hot in a sports bra and the type of spandex short-shorts that would've given both my parents a heart attack.

[About to go for a run.]

[Want to come over in about an hour? We're gonna have a BBQ.]

Oh my gosh, that sounded like so much fun!

[Are you sure? I wouldn't want to impose…]

[Do I need to spank you again already?]

All right, now *that*, had me choking on the saliva I'd just worked up to remoisten my mouth.

Good thing vampires didn't need to breathe.

I must have spent way too long reading and rereading Morgan's message, trying to think of something witty to reply with, because the next thing I knew, those three blinking dots had appeared again.

[Well?]

My traitorous fingers had already typed out, *[Yes please!]* before I managed to reel myself in and revise my reply to a much less embarrassing, *[I'll be there!]*

[Good girl. <3]

Those two simple words and their emoji heart literally had me swooning, and I had to grab hold of the bathroom sink to keep from falling. While I was busy doing that, Morgan sent me her address. And, checking the time on my phone, I did some quick mental math before misting over to the oven and setting it to preheat to 350.

"All right! I'll change into something cute, pop by the store for some light thieving, come back and bake up a storm, and then be at Morgan's in no time. Yes! Let's do this!"

One thing I was not at all prepared for when I stepped out from the shadow cast by the streetlight in front of Morgan's house was just how big it was. I hadn't really been paying much attention when I'd beat my hasty retreat last time, so I'd been expecting something more along the lines of a rundown college rental, not... Well, it looked like it could be a sorority house with the number of rooms it apparently had.

"Heh. That'd definitely explain her interest in spanking."

Following the sounds of laughter coming from behind the house, I tugged down on the hem of my slightly too short to be totally modest dress and wove my way between a pair of very fast looking motorcycles and a mud-splattered jeep, before deciding that I was probably out of sight enough to mist my way onto the other side of the fence. There, I stood perfectly still beside the water meter and tried to get my bearings, all the while silently berating myself for not just knocking on the front door like a normal person.

Oh well, I was there now, and I wasn't about to turn back.

I was sick of running.

The back yard itself was just as big as the house was, with a huge deck and a wide stretch of just starting to go dormant grass. Tatiana and another girl with bright blonde curls I didn't recognize were currently sprinting back and forth across it, chucking what I assumed was a lacrosse ball at each other with reckless abandon. And, like, *wow*. Were they on the university's team or something? They definitely seemed like they'd be a serious threat out on the field (pitch?), judging by the way they were grunting and growling at each other every time they snapped their net-stick things forward.

Before I could dwell too long on how cute it was that two

werewolves were having so much fun chasing a ball around their back yard, a broad-shouldered woman in khaki shorts and a partially-unbuttoned Hawaiian shirt in front of a massive grill waved to me with her spatula.

"Hey there! You must be Melody. Morgan'll be back in just a bit. Come keep me company until then, yeah?"

"Sure!" Misting over to right beside her without warning, hoping to make her jump, I flashed the woman a fangy grin. "Hi!"

She didn't even flinch.

Rude. "Hey yourself. I'm Dorian," she said instead, pulling me into a firm side hug with her free hand. "It's nice to finally meet you. The boss has been going on and on about you all week."

"Oh! Um, you too," I squeaked, my face flushing with a warmth that had nothing to do with the heat from the propane grill in front of us as I was smooshed against the deceptively large breasts hidden beneath the loose folds of Dorian's top. "Er, I mean- She hasn't mentioned *you*, but- Er..."

Forcing myself to blow out a breath so I could stop babbling, I opted for a self-deprecating smile instead.

"Uh, yeah. It's nice to meet you too."

"Awww, you're just cute as a button, ain't ya?"

One corner of Dorian's mouth twitched up as she said that, revealing a hint of pointed teeth as she let me go.

"Um, thanks?"

"You're welcome!"

Ugh. Why am I so freaking awkward?

Without Morgan's effortless confidence to lean on / hide behind, I was all too aware of just how absurdly out of my depth I was right then. Even before I'd been turned, I'd never been very good at social gatherings, let alone had a pretty girl invite me over to her place for a barbecue with all her cool werewolf friends. What were we even supposed to talk about? The moon?

Eager to change the topic, I latched onto the first thing that came to mind and leaned forward to take in a deep breath of the sizzling meat on the grill in front of us.

"Oh, wow, that smells *really* good."

"I know, right?" Dorian's chest puffed out with pride as she spoke. "It's bear!"

"Oooh, that's fun. I didn't even know you could buy bear."

"Mmmm, yeah, try again on that one, sweetheart."

"Wait, you can? I thought the fanciest thing the grocery sold were those pre-cooked rotisserie chicken things."

At that, Dorian tipped back her head and let loose with a deep belly laugh.

"God, you are just precious." This time, the smile she flashed me was chock full of very pointy teeth as her hazel eyes flashed a luminous gold. "I took this bad boy down myself last week when we were out hunting."

She was practically drooling now as she licked her lips.

"I just got him back from the butcher today. I'd have prepped him myself, but Morgan says she doesn't want the kitchen looking like a crime scene," she added with a put-upon huff that was honestly pretty cute in a scary sort of way. "So, you more of a burger or a steak girl? We've got plenty of both, so pick whatever you want, yeah?"

Before I could reply, Dorian slapped herself on the forehead.

"Oh crap, my bad," she apologized with a shake of her head. "I forgot you're a vamp for a second there. So, uh, do you still, you know…"

She made a vague, swirling gesture with her spatula.

"Yep." Nodding quickly, I did my best to reassure her with a broad smile that showed off my fangs. "I don't actually need to eat regular food anymore since the only thing that actually keeps me satiated is fresh blood, but it's still fun to shake things up every now and then. I would absolutely love a burger, please."

I was starting salivate just a bit myself.

"Those look yummy as heck."

"You got it. One bear burger for Morgan's favorite bare bottom brat coming right up."

Dorian winked at me as she said that, and there was something almost deferential about it even as it set my face aflame all over again.

"I-! That's not-! She-!"

I didn't have long to splutter, though, before Tatiana and her lacrosse partner came rushing up the deck to crowd with us around the grill.

"So, is new girl eating or what?" the blonde asked.

"Yep! She apparently lusts after my quality cooking just as much as Tatiana's B positive."

I squirmed a little at the light teasing, especially when Tatiana winked at me.

"OMG, your fangs are so *cute*!" the wolf I hadn't met yet exclaimed then, slipping her lithe frame in front of me in the blink of an eye as she brought her bright green and gold eyes only a couple of inches away from my mouth. "Oh!"

Before looking up at me, only mildly chagrined.

"I'm Sasha. Nice to meet you," she added, before going back to eyeballing my fangs.

"Whoa there, down girl. Morgan's already claimed her, remember?" Tatiana said with a smirk, dragging the bubbly blonde back by the scruff of her neck.

"Ahhh, don't be such a spoil spot, T. There's no harm in a tiny taste."

That had all three of them snorting out a laugh. "Okay, now you *know* that's not true."

SMACK! SMACK!

Sasha danced from foot to foot with the pair of heavy-handed swats that Tatiana delivered to the seat of her shorts, before crossing her arms beneath the modest swell of her breasts with a pout that didn't quite manage to reach her smiling eyes.

"You're a total fun suck, you know that?"

"Oh, don't be such a baby," Tatiana soothed, kissing the scowl off the shorter wolf's lips. "You've been waving that thing at me all night."

"Yep!" Back to being chipper, Sasha giggled. "Took you long enough."

"Careful..." warned Tatiana in a teasing drawl. "I could always bend you over right now and show the new girl just how well you color up. We've got enough time before the food's ready, right Dorian?"

"Sure do," confirmed the cook with a grin.

"Promises, promises." Completely undeterred by the threat of a public spanking, Sasha captured Tatiana's lips in another kiss, nipping at her lower lip and flipping off Dorian as she drew back enough to smirk in self-satisfaction.

"You are so getting it later," growled Tatiana playfully, somehow making the act of rubbing noses with the blonde seem downright menacing. "I'm talking plug, paddle, strap, no warm up, the works. You're going to be a fucking *wreck* when we're through with you."

Sighing happily, Sasha melted against her front with a soft smile.

"You know just what a girl loves to hear, don't you?"

"Damn right I do, baby."

Grateful for the distraction, even as my lower abdomen stirred at the casual display of dominance going on in front of me, I thrust the plastic container I'd been holding onto that entire time toward Tatiana before my blush could push its way up to the roots of my hair.

"I made these for you!" I squeaked, feeling like a total dork. "Um, you know, as a thank you... for the other night..."

Tatiana kept me standing there with my arms thrust forward while she and her fellow wolves let out simultaneous "Awww"s, before taking pity on me enough to accept the gift and pop open the lid.

"Fuck me, that is a lot of calories," she said with an impressed whistle before plucking up one of the homemade devil's food and vanilla cream cheese frosting cookie sandwiches from their wax paper lining and taking a bite that resulted in a downright lascivious moan.

Her reaction immediately had the other two snatching up their own cookie sandwiches, each with similar reactions as they bit into them.

"OMG YUMMY!"

"Yeah, no wonder Morgan's been all over her. Cute tits, spank-able ass, *and* talent in the kitchen? Talk about a triple threat."

Well. Guess I was just going to be blushing all night then. Cool.

"Heh, thanks…" I demurred, tucking some of my hair behind an ear and wishing suddenly that I'd hopped into the shower before coming over. "My mom and I used to bake these all the time for church activities when I was growing up, so I got a lot of practice in over the years."

"You have got to give me your recipe, these are amazing," Dorian insisted, grabbing another cookie.

"Totally!" agreed Sasha, ducking in between the bigger wolf's arms to steal a bite since she'd already devoured hers.

Dorian took it right back, though, when she fisted a handful of her curls and wrenched her head back and to the side to roughly kiss her.

Positively glowing with pride now, I didn't even hesitate to turn to Tatiana and ask, "Wait, I thought you two were dating?" nodding toward where Sasha and Dorian were now aggressively making out while Dorian continued to flip the meat on the grill beside her with her spatula.

That must've been a funny question to ask, because Dorian, Sasha, and Tatiana all broke down in yet more laughter.

"Come on, y'all, be nice," Dorian halfheartedly chided the other two. "Morgan said she's an innocent little lamb, remember?"

"Yeah, yeah…"

Not even a little bit chastened, Tatiana rolled her eyes, while Sasha shot me a wicked grin.

"We *are* dating," she said with a breathy gasp as Dorian slipped her free hand down the back of her shorts and Tatiana reached around the petite girl's front to fondle her breasts. "We're in a- Mmph! In a triad."

"Um, like that gang in Rush Hour?"

Apparently, they were not, in fact, part of a Hong Kong crime syndicate, because they once again dissolved into hysterical laughter.

"No, you goofball," came the deep timbre of Morgan's own chuckling reply from out of the blue then as her strong arms enveloped me in a hug from behind. "They're in a polyamorous relationship. They're *all* dating each other."

"Ooooh!" And here I was thinking that Morgan and I were the height of kinky daring with her spanking me out in semi-public that one time. "That sounds a lot more fun than the crappy version Mormons used to do."

This time, we all laughed, and I felt the knot of anxiety inside my stomach unravel all at once. This was fun!

"Please tell me you're keeping her, Morgan," Dorian said, feigning wiping a tear from her eye.

"Yep. She's all mine." Morgan pulled me in against her as she spoke, leaning down to nuzzle her cheek against mine. Fresh from her run, the heated iron curves of her slightly sweaty body molded themselves to my soft physique; bleeding heat into my chilled frame as her heady scent of pine needles and something spicy wrapped around me like my favorite childhood blanket. "I'm totally head over heels for my sweet Melody."

"Me too," I sighed, smiling dreamily up at her over my shoulder, feeling safe and secure, and utterly content.

"Awww," cooed Sasha.

While Tatiana added sotto voce, "More like she's going to be heels over head before the night is through."

"Hmmm, nah. With hips like that, it'll be head down, ass up, maybe hands tied behind her back," mused Dorian. "There are all sorts of fun options, aren't there, Melody?"

"I- I- Um-!"

"Shhh, pet. That was a rhetorical question," Morgan soothed.

I could practically feel the savage grin pulling at the corners of her lips as she nipped at my ear before mercifully changing the subject from what position she wanted to put me in before the night was through. "We ready to eat yet? I'm starved."

A lot of those steaks looked pretty rare to me, but Dorian still nodded.

"Just about," she said, giving a couple of the burger patties a flip with an offhand flick of her wrist. "Dani said she'll be down in a few. She's still cramming for her midterm. So, if you want to go ahead and get you and your lady settled, I'll make up a plate for each of you."

"You don't have to-" I started to protest, before being just as quickly cut off by Morgan nipping at my ear again as she started dragging me off toward a glass-topped outdoor table further down the deck.

"Sounds like a plan. Thanks!"

My bear burger tasted even better than it smelled, albeit spicier than I'd expected it to be. Still, it was yummy, and I wound up putting back two of them without even thinking about it while Morgan and her pack demolished a borderline absurd amount of very rare steaks.

Apparently, I wasn't the only one who enjoyed a bit of blood for dinner.

At some point, Sasha ducked back into the big house before returning with an acoustic guitar, much to the excitement of Tatiana and Dorian. Her strumming soon became a relaxing backdrop as we settled in around the fire pit that acted as the focal point for the expansive deck, content to let our stomachs digest while we chatted lazily and enjoyed each other's company. Without even realizing I'd done it, I'd somehow become just another part of the group (well, pack, I guess), and I was feeling about a million times more relaxed than I had been when I first arrived as Morgan settled me on top of her lap, her strong arms draping around my waist to hold me close. Letting me know without words that I was safe. That I was *hers*.

This was nice.

This was... home?

Whatever it was, I never wanted it to end.

"Basically, Mom and I decided that the pack was in danger of turning into a bunch of feral mountain hermits in another two or three generations if we didn't start pushing our younger wolves to integrate into society by getting some sort of post-secondary school education," Morgan was explaining to me, playing with my hair while we cuddled.

"You mean to tell me there aren't a bunch of secret werewolf business bros out there starting app ventures?" I yawned, tracing patterns across the material of the sports bra Morgan was wearing as a top.

For someone who was half naked just then (she only had on a skimpy pair of running shorts and a pair of well-worn tennis shoes to accompany the bra), she seemed to run surprisingly hot. Even with the heat from the fire pit, her body was positively radiating warmth like she was her own personal furnace. Which was good, because one thing that Hollywood had managed to get right about us vampires was that we are a very chilly bunch of bloodsuckers.

"There're a few, but not as many as we'd like," Dani said, breaking me away from my contemplation of how comfortable Morgan was as she looked up from the game she was playing on her phone. "Our main compound is way up in the Rockies, so it's easy to feel like all you need to be good at is running down prey and keeping the borders secure."

"Isolationism isn't exactly viable in this day and age, though," added Tatiana.

"Mmhmm."

Morgan paused to take a deep inhale of my hair before giving my hips a possessive squeeze.

"So, I decided we needed to set up a sister pack somewhere not in the middle of nowhere. And, well, since I already wanted to get my PhD in art history anyway, Mom and I picked out a few volunteers to keep me company as we got things going, and then we bought this place so pack members would always have somewhere safe to stay while going to school or working in the city."

"That's… surprisingly forward thinking," I mused, nibbling at my thumbnail while I tried to imagine what it would be like to grow up so far away from modern society. I mean, don't get me wrong, I'm a total indoor kid, but I still liked having the option to meet other people from time to time.

Of course, it was only after I'd let that thought wander out that it occurred to me what I'd just said.

"Oh, crap! I'm sorry, I didn't mean to imply-!"

Before I could finish my apology, though, Morgan cut me off with a kiss.

"I know," she said with a couple firm pats to the top of one thigh that had my stomach lurching with a sudden burst of sense memory from the other night.

"Um, uh, r-right."

Swallowing my embarrassment, I flashed her a shy smile, grateful for her understanding.

"God, you're cute," she sighed, nuzzling her cheek against mine.

"And you're pretty," I countered, my smile brightening in the subdued glow of the fire pit.

I really loved how cuddly she was. You'd think someone so strong and effortlessly in command wouldn't be so physically affectionate, but apparently it was just one of those werewolf things. Dani, Dorian, Tatiana, and Sasha, for instance, had been all over each other ever since we'd sat down to eat. Constantly exchanging small, lingering touches, sometimes seemingly without even realizing they were doing it.

It was downright heartwarming.

"So, what about you, Mel?" prompted Sasha, still strumming away at her guitar as she openly ogled where the hem of my dress had risen more than halfway up my thighs, exposing an expanse of moon pale skin and the snug tops of my black stockings. "What do you want to be when you grow up? Queen of a haunted castle? Shadowy information broker? Oh, oh! How about a manager at a rave club? I hear you rock a mean pair of leather pants."

"I've thought about the vampire queen thing more than a little bit," I admitted with an unabashed giggle. "I mean, really, how could I not? It would be almost criminal not to, right?"

"Seriously! Can you even call yourself a vampire if you don't have at least one sex dungeon?"

"I, um-!" I stuttered, the tips of my ears going molten lava hot. "I guess not. Heh."

"You are so lucky you don't have a seethe," Morgan said with a bemused shake of her head. "I can guarantee your sire would absolutely obliterate that bratty butt of yours if they heard you talking like that."

"So you're saying I *shouldn't* mention the cape I bought on Amazon last week if I ever run into her?"

"Probably not, no."

"Or, if you do," added Sasha. "Make sure to tell me first so I can get a good seat for the show."

"Okay, you two are a bad influence on each other and I love it." Shaking her head, Morgan blew out an amused sigh. "Seriously, though, Melody, what *do* you want to do with your unlife? You're basically immortal now. Surely, you must have some sort of dream? A goal you want to accomplish?"

"Well..."

Hesitating, my cheeks warmed again and I suddenly became very preoccupied with adjusting my position on top of Morgan's lap.

"Spill it," she ordered, refusing to let me wriggle my way out of answering her question either literally or figuratively.

"Okay, fine." I channeled my embarrassment at being put on the spot into an extra-pouty huff, which just made Morgan smile in that way that made me want to simultaneously stomp her foot and never stop kissing her. "I want to open a retro computing museum."

"Oooh. Like the big one they have over in the UK?" asked Dani, suddenly perking up.

"Yes, exactly! Oh my gosh you're the first person I've ever met in real life who's heard of that!"

I was all but bouncing in place on top of Morgan's lap at the unexpected interest in my idea. Normally, whenever I brought it up with Mom or Dad, I was either hit with a dismissive, "Huh. That's interesting," or the even more annoying, "And how are you supposed to pay the bills doing that?" If it wasn't about MLMs or real estate investing, my parents automatically assumed it was a bad idea.

They aren't here now, though, are they? So screw them.

"Basically, I want to do what they have in Swindon, but with, like, a bunch more interactive areas," I started to explain. "I want people to be able to pull up a seat and be able to experience what it was like to actually use the exhibits when they first came out back in the day, instead of just looking at them collecting dust behind some display case."

"Yes, yes, yes! I *love* that." Dani was bouncing just as much as I was now. "That sounds like so much fun."

"I know, right? I especially would want to get an early nineties area going. That was such a fascinating time for performance jumps and 3D standardization!" Letting out a wistful sigh as my initial burst of excitement petered out into the inevitable disappointment that followed whenever I thought too much about my museum dream, I relaxed back against Morgan's chest. "That's actually why I'm majoring in business management. My dad said I needed to get a 'real' degree if he and Mom were going to pay for school, and it seemed like a close enough fit for what I wanted to do. Not that it really matters now, I guess."

"What? Why?" demanded Morgan. "Who's stopping you?"

The way she asked that last question carried with it an implicit threat that if I gave her a name, she'd make whoever was standing in my pay dearly. Which was both incredibly touching, and also kind of scary in an exciting sort of way.

"I mean… Me? I guess? I'm taking remote classes right now since I can't drop out without explaining things to my parents, and daytime courses are a nonstarter, obviously. But, even if I graduate, I still have no idea what I'm actually going to do for a job.

"I guess I could maybe work remotely or something, but there's no way I'd ever make enough money doing that to get a museum off the ground. Trust me, I've checked. Renting big commercial spaces is not at all cheap. Plus, like, what would I even do if I *did* somehow get it going? It would be kind of hard to run something like that while being dead to the world during business hours, wouldn't it?"

Rather than berate me for being such a downer, Morgan just gave me another squeeze and nuzzled my cheek.

"I'm sorry you've had to deal with those feelings all by yourself," she murmured softly, sending shivers down my spine before raising her voice again. "But this is exactly the kind of shit I had in mind when I started this satellite pack. Wolves, *and* vampires, let's be real, need to get their collective asses into the twenty-first century already. So, if that's really what you want, I'm sure we can figure out something for you eventually."

"Wait, really?" Now that just about managed to stop my undead heart. "But, why? I'm not even a wolf."

"You're my mate, dingbat," Morgan chided me with a loving smile. "That makes you part of the pack."

"Oh. Um… I… I see."

Mate?

That definitely sounded a lot more serious than just girlfriend. Not that I exactly minded, per se. Still, we were going to have to talk about that sooner or later. For now, though, I was content to just go with the flow and be her mate. Whatever that meant.

It felt pretty nice, actually.

"You know…" piped up Dani then, grinning at me from

across the fire pit. "If you want, we could play pretend in my room until you can get the real thing going. It's like forty percent loose motherboards and half-finished restoration projects right now anyway."

"Really?" I asked, my lips automatically pulling back to mirror her grin.

"Oh yeah. I've got three different half-dead Amigas that I've been trying to Frankenstein together into at least one or two working units off and on between classes for the last couple months, and I could really use a hand with recapping them."

"That would be awesome!" I exclaimed, back to bouncing. "Are you going to retrobright them?"

"Of course. Can't have yellowed plastics, now can I?"

"Heck yes! I've got, like, a dozen bottles of hydrogen peroxide you can have if you want," I offered in a rush.

"Really?" Dani's eyes were flashing a bright gold now. "You sure you don't mind?"

"Not at all. I can't really retrobright anything myself anymore, since, you know, vampires and UV rays don't mix. They're all yours if you want them."

"Wow, thanks! That'd be great!"

"Awww, listen to the nerds nerding it up," teased Dorian, leaning over to affectionately nip at Dani, earning herself a friendly punch to the arm in return.

For my part, I harrumphed good-naturedly at her, folding my arms across my breasts and shifting my position on Morgan's lap so that it felt more like a throne instead of my mate / girlfriend's crazy firm thighs.

"I'll have you know that this nerd could kick your butt without even trying," I sneered, making a show of imperiously crossing one leg over the other.

"Oh yeah?" countered Dorian, eyes shining just as golden as Dani's as her mouth pulled back into a feral grin. "Care to prove that... *nerd*?"

"Bring it!"

CHAPTER 8

Melody

The next thing I knew, I was being dragged (quite literally, Dorian was *very* insistent) into an arm wrestling contest between me and everyone else in the pack. Well, everyone except for Morgan, who seemed content to act as a lap for me to sit on while I competed. And, while every wolf I faced was absurdly toned with steel bands of sinewy muscle lurking just beneath their tanned, olive skin, even petite Sasha who I suspected was probably at the bottom of the pecking (biting?) order based on how everyone else seemed so comfortable with slapping her on the butt, I still managed to trounce all of them without breaking so much as a sweat.

Not that I really did much sweating these days to begin with, but you know what I mcan.

Regardless of how much perspiration was involved, I still made sure to let each of them put in a good performance as we leaned over the table we'd been eating at earlier, our hands clasped together and either Dorian or Dani acting as judge. I'd feign a yawn or maybe pretend to check my social feeds whilc they gritted their teeth and strained as hard as they could to get me to budge, before then springing into action and taking them down in one smooth push that actually managed to send Dani toppling out of her chair once (to the raucous laughter and friendly ribbing of her fellow wolves).

Honestly, it was a lot of fun being the toughest one in the group for a change.

I should have known it wouldn't last.

"What do you say, Morgan? Care to try your luck?" I found myself wheedling after thoroughly trouncing every other wolf in her pack at least three more times, wiggling my hips against her lap for added incentive. "I promise I'll go easy on you if you ask me nicely."

"Hmmm... Pretty sure you're already intimately familiar with how strong my arm is, batty buns," my mate countered lazily, her lips twitching up just enough to show off the points of her teeth.

"No I'm not!" I started to protest, before dissolving into a cascade of tingling shivers as her hands glided down the sides of my dress, her fingers playing along its tautly stretched hem as they settled against where my hips spilled out over either side of her lap.

"Of course, if you need a reminder," she murmured against my ear in that way I instinctively knew spelled trouble (and which, ironically enough, made me want to go sprinting headfirst into it). "I'd be more than happy to turn you over my knee again right now. Weren't you saying last time that you wished you had someone there to watch me blister your bare bottom while you begged for mercy?"

"I...! Um, that's not-! You don't have to-"

I was pretty sure I could actually feel Morgan's nails sharpening into claws as she dug them in against my flanks, piercing through the material of my dress and literally pinning me in place.

"While we're at it, we could also show off how, ahem, *accommodating* your little ass pucker is," she added in a taunting singsong, grinding me against her groin with a low chuckle. "That is... if you ask me nicely."

She kissed my cheek then, and there was no way everyone

couldn't see just how wet I'd become since my thighs had apparently decided to spread themselves as wide as they would go while I hadn't been paying attention. Pushing my dress further up to expose the sheer gusset and scalloped frills of my panties in a shameless plea for Morgan to touch me there.

"Fuck her, fuck her!" chanted Dorian, Tatiana, and Sasha together, while Dani choked on the beer she'd been drinking before joining in.

In that moment, I knew I should at least make an attempt to climb out of the hole I'd managed to dig for myself, that I was playing with fire the more I kept taunting my mate. But, egged on by the salivating whoops and catcalls from my appreciative audience, I ignored every self-preservation instinct I still had left and plowed straight ahead with the first sassy thing that sprang to mind. Which, believe it or not, turned out to be a mistake.

At least it was the fun kind.

"Awww, what's the matter, Morgan? Don't tell me the big bad Alpha is afraid of looking like a noodly arm baby in front of all her friends?" I gave a mocking pout before flashing the taller girl a fangy grin that did absolutely nothing to distract from how my stomach was roiling with about a million panicking bats in search of shelter from my no doubt looming comeuppance. "Weren't *you* the one who was all out of breath and complaining that her shoulder was hurting after we were through the other night?"

"Ooooh!" sang the peanut gallery then, four pairs of luminous golden eyes and way too wide grins glowing in the shadows cast by the fire pit.

Oh my gosh, what the heck am I doing?

"Oh, darn. I guess I'm just going to have to teach you a lesson after all, pet," droned Morgan, not sounding particularly upset all things considered as she relaxed back into her seat and hit me with a look that had the little hairs on the back of my neck to standing on end.

Uh-oh.

"Dani," she crooned, keeping me transfixed with her glowing

eyes and predator's smile. "Be a dear and go grab one of my belts and that necklace we were talking about, would you?"

"Oh hell yes! You got it, girl!"

Bouncing up from her seat, Dani offered Morgan a crisp salute (a closed fist rapped twice against her left collarbone) and favored me with a lascivious wink, before sprinting back inside the house.

"Um… Necklace?"

While my spanking experience growing up might have been limited to a wooden paddle with CTR emblazoned onto it (which my parents, no joke, actually made me keep on a hook beside my bedroom door all the way through high school since I "needed an extra incentive to choose the right", blech!), I could still hazard a guess as to what the belt was for. The jewelry, on the other hand, was a total mystery.

"You'll see soon enough," Morgan promised, her hypnotic gaze swirling with a mixture of vindictive resolve and sadistic glee that only served to further soak the front of my panties.

Then, quick as a flash, her hand was fisted around my hair and she was dragging me to my feet where she captured my startled lips in a savage, hungry kiss. It was rough and possessive, and as she slanted her mouth against mine, shoving her tongue in past my fangs, I felt all the fight drain from my body as I melted into her embrace.

This was right.

This was how it was supposed to be.

And, oh my *freaking* gosh, how was she so good at kissing?

"Morgan, please…" I whimpered when she drew back from me to catch her breath, my hands clenching and unclenching at my sides as I fought the urge to reach beneath my dress or else go for her jugular. "You can't-"

Before I could figure out what I was actually complaining about (the impending spanking, or her not helping me come right that second), I was silenced by a surprisingly soft pair of fingertips being pressed to my lips for the second time that night.

"Hush," she ordered in a voice that brooked no argument. "And strip."

"Strip?!" I squeaked, disobeying her in record time as my face flushed a shade of red I was pretty sure was even brighter than my hair.

"You wanted to show off for the girls, didn't you?" Morgan asked with a saccharine sweetness that made my legs go to jelly. "Well, congratulations, now you get to show everyone just how tasty those curves of yours are."

"Seems like a great idea to me."

Nodding sagely, Tatiana licked her lips while Sasha belted out a dramatic riff on her guitar before setting it aside and moving to plop down on top of her lap.

"Sorry, not sorry, Mel," she chirped, her pointed canines flashing at me in the firelight. "You really should know better than to go challenging the Alpha for dominance like that."

"I wasn't-" I started to protest.

"Yes." Morgan cut me off with another (much harder) squeeze to my hair. "You were."

"Ah! Okay, okay, so I might have *maybe* been challenging you," I conceded through clenched teeth, easing onto my tiptoes to lessen some of the pressure on my scalp while holding up a hand, forefinger and thumb an inch or so apart. "In my defense, though, it was just an itsy bitsy one."

That managed to get my mate chuckling.

"An 'itsy bitsy' one is all it takes."

She nipped at my ear then, sending tidal waves of tingles across the side of my face where her breath tickled my hypersensitive skin, before releasing me with the sort of smirk that made it abundantly clear that she knew exactly how much she was embarrassing me and loved every second of it just as much as I was.

"Thanks for that, by the way," Tatiana added while she snaked a hand down the front of Sasha's shorts.

"Yeah, seriously," the blonde agreed, her head tipping back with a gasp. "Oh god, r-right there, babe. Don't… Don't stop…"

Doing my best not to think too hard about what was going on beneath those shorts lest my face really did burst into flames, I cast a pleading look back toward Morgan. I could tell by the way she arched a single, questioning brow at me that she wouldn't make me take my clothes off in front of the others if I didn't want to. It wouldn't get me out of my spanking, I was sure (and I wouldn't have wanted it to anyway), but it was still nice to know that she cared enough about my feelings to offer me at least a sliver of an out.

Good thing for both of us, then, that all I wanted to do was exactly as I was told.

"All right, I suppose I see your point," I said, playing it up for our audience as I let loose with an elaborate sigh. Then, before my nerve and absolutely rampant horniness could fail me, I reached for the hem of my dress and tugged it inside-out up and over my head in one smooth motion. Dropping it onto the chair that Morgan and I had just abandoned with a dismissive toss of my hair. "There. Happy now?"

"Extremely."

Morgan's ravenous gaze scorched its way across every square inch of milky white skin not currently being covered by my stockings or the matching bra and panty set I'd picked out for tonight just in case I found myself in a situation like this (though, at the time, I'd only pictured it being the two of us), and it was all I could do not to crumble under its relentless pressure as it zeroed in on my chest.

"Now, ditch the rest before I do it for you."

"I, um..."

The way she bore her teeth at me as she said that painted an *extremely* vivid mental image of her using those wicked looking claws now tipping her fingers to rip my underwear to shreds before ravishing me in front of her pack mates. And, oh my gosh, oh my dang, I was so tempted to call her bluff.

"Yes ma'am."

In the end, though, the lingering vestiges of my Mormon upbringing won out over my burgeoning exhibitionist streak, and I reached behind me with slightly trembling hands to undo the clasp on the back of my bra.

The quiet gasp that escaped from Morgan and the others as my breasts bounced free from their partially see-through confines a moment later, their peachy tips straining for her attention, was extremely satisfying. And the low growl coupled with the menacing step she took toward me as I hooked my thumbs into either side of my panties and pushed them (along with my stockings) all the way down to my ankles was more than enough to make the no doubt extremely unpleasant bottom blistering I still had coming totally worth it.

Where the heck has this crazy confident, sexy Melody been hiding all this time?

I guess she'd just been waiting for her mate.

"What the fuck, Morgan, she's so hotttt," Dorian moaned from behind me, sounding absurdly jealous as she tossed an empty beer can over my head at her Alpha in protest. "*Please* take me with you the next time you and Dani go out."

Sasha, meanwhile, let out a high-pitched squeal.

"Holy shit, is that what I think it is?"

"Huh? What?" I asked, turning in circles (and only stumbling a little over the pile of discarded clothes at my feet) as I tried to figure out what she was pointing at before remembering the teeth marks contrasting sharply against the pale skin of my shoulder in a lurid display of dark purple. "Oh, hey, yeah! I was wondering why that was taking so long to heal."

"It's a mate bite." Morgan looked extremely pleased with herself as she delivered that particular bit of news. "It doesn't fade and it doesn't heal. Even for vampires."

"OMG, your mom is going to freak!"

"Already told her." Morgan shrugged, still beaming. "She and Mama are very excited."

"I'll just bet she is," snickered Tatiana, sharing a wry look with Dorian. "Has she and Kate started picking out names for grandkids yet?"

To which my mate gave a rueful laugh.

"Oh, I'm sure they have."

While I somehow managed to pale even further.

"I… I, well, uh," I stuttered, only just now managing to find my voice again.

Grandkids? Seriously?

That was a lot to take in, even if neither of us had ready access to sperm, making it kind of a moot point. But, again, I decided that I might as well just go with the flow since the idea of being bound to Morgan via some sort of werewolf marriage pact didn't really sound all that awful. (It sounded pretty nice, actually.) Whatever I might have been roped into, we could sort out the details later. For now, rather than freak out, I instead flashed Morgan a fangy grin and lightly fingered the bruises at the crook of my neck.

"These are definitely a lot cooler than some boring old ring, that's for sure." Before a jolt of worried realization shot through me, and I added in a rush, "Wait. This isn't going to turn me into a werewolf, is it? Er… a were-pire?"

Thankfully, Morgan just laughed and shook her head.

"Nope, that's hereditary, I'm afraid," she explained, before yanking me in against her front by my soon to be spanked backside. "All that bite does is let everybody know that you're *mine*."

Underscoring just what she meant, she brought her lips to mine in a prolonged, passionate kiss. Pushing her tongue inside my mouth at the same time that she slipped a thigh between my legs.

"Mmph!"

And, just like that, my brain fuzzed out into a white fog of blissful oblivion as I came like a tsunami right there in her arms. My mate refusing to let me go as she fed on the moans working to escape from our locked lips.

"Music to my ears," Morgan rumbled, letting me go as I struggled to claw my way through a thick morass of knee-wobbling pleasure, arousal slicking the insides of my trembling thighs. "Sasha, get T's fingers out of your snatch and go cut me some switches. You know the kind I like."

"Awww, do I have to?"

"Yes."

"Better hurry if you don't want to be cutting two sets," Tatiana murmured against the side of the shorter girl's neck before withdrawing her hand from the front of her shorts.

"Humph. Fiiiine."

Rather than blush tomato red like I definitely would have in her position, Sasha instead slipped off of Tatiana's lap with a roll of her eyes, and then went skipping out into the darkness toward a pair of crepe myrtles near the back end of the yard.

"Um, switches?" I squeaked, Morgan's words finally pushing past my brain fog enough to register.

"Yep. Figure we might as well take advantage of them while they're still in season."

"I mean… Strong disagree, but you do you, I guess."

"I was planning on doing *you*, actually," Morgan corrected, gliding a palm down the soft, smooth skin of my stomach before very nearly knocking my knees out from under me again as she dipped two fingers between my thighs to part my sopping folds.

"Oh m-my go- Ah!"

"Damn, sensitive much?" marveled Dorian.

"Mmhmm."

Morgan underscored her agreement by working a finger in past my opening and curling it against a nerve cluster inside of me that had me collapsing against her with a startled cry as I was caught up in the throes of yet another orgasm.

"Talk about a hair trigger," laughed Tatiana from her spot beside the broad-shouldered woman.

"She says it's a vampire thing," Morgan explained, all the while continuing to finger me, heedless of my whimpering moans as I rode out the bone-rattling tremors of one climax into the next without any time to catch my (thankfully unnecessary) breath, my face buried against her chest where her blood sang to me just beneath her skin. “My guess is that whatever venom she injects with her bite that makes you come while she’s chowing down is also pumping through her system all the time as well, and she’s just developed a tolerance for it.”

Right on cue, I squealed and my legs gave out from under me, forcing her to reach down and hold me up by my backside with her free hand.

“Well, a partial tolerance,” she amended. “Either way, it’s a total ego boost.”

I clung desperately to the deep rumble of Morgan’s laughter as it reverberated through where our bodies were pressed together, using it as an anchor to keep myself at least somewhat grounded to reality.

“Pretty sure she’s going to explode when I finally get around to fucking her properly.”

The way she said that only added to my confusion, since I’d been under the impression that we already *had* been having sex. Like, I mean, she had her fingers inside of me right that second, didn’t she?

I didn’t really get a chance to mull that one over, though, because just as I was starting to come back to reality, Dani emerged from the house amid a triumphant cheer from her fellow wolves.

“Got ‘em!” she declared, waving her prizes above her head for all to see.

“Hell yeah. Thanks, girl.”

Pulling free from between my legs with the sort of wet squelching noise that elevated my embarrassment from all consuming to borderline terminal, Morgan accepted the belt and necklace with a nod of thanks and then took a step back, the corner of her mouth quirking up into a playful half-grin.

"All right, my sweet Melody, we're going to try a little experiment. Put your wrists together for me, like this."

She demonstrated what she wanted me to do, clasping her own hands together as if in prayer. And, after a brief moment of hesitation, not really sure why she would want my hands up in front of my chest like that, I obeyed.

"Good girl," she cooed as she began wrapping a length of delicate silver links around my wrists once, twice, and then three times, binding them together just snugly enough that they wouldn't be able to pull away from each other. "Now, for the belt."

Again, she bound my wrists together, wrapping the well-worn strip of thick black leather around them a couple times before securing it in place with its shiny silver buckle.

"Perfect."

"So, uh…" I ventured tentatively while I watched her give her handiwork a pleased once-over. "Not that I don't like the idea of being tied up by you and all," and oh boy did I ever, I realized with a start as a fresh ache began to bubble up between my legs. "But, you do know I'm still a vampire, right?"

"Kinda hard to forget," mumbled Tatiana, rubbing at the side of her neck where I'd bitten her.

Morgan, though, didn't look worried.

"Go ahead and try to break out of them," she challenged, eyes flickering in amusement.

"Okay," I said with a shrug. "Don't say I didn't warn you, though."

Given the greenlight to break my mate's stuff, I flexed my forearms and pulled at my wrists. Only, instead of the expected snapping of both leather and chain, my wrists remained bound together right where they were.

"Um…"

I tried again, pouring all of my strength into the action this time. Which felt mildly ridiculous given the fact that I was completely naked just then.

Still nothing.

"What the-?" I started to demand, my stomach lurching with a brand new surge of fear and excitement.

"Silver necklace."

Morgan spoke those two words with such self-satisfied glee that I was surprised she hadn't thrown her head back to cackle while she did it. Instead, she reached out and gave one of my erect nipples a light twist that blanked out my mind for a good three seconds, nearly making me come all over again.

"The silver neutralizes your vampiric strength," she explained with a languid sort of sadistic glee, taking hold of my other nipple with her free hand and dragging me toward her until I was forced to look up to meet her gaze. "And the belt keeps your hands right where I want them since even at your baseline human strength you could probably still break that necklace."

She swallowed the cry of exquisite pain and ecstasy that welled up inside my throat as she gave both my nipples the sort of hard pinch that had me seeing stars by crashing her snarling mouth into mine in a savage kiss that literally left me breathless.

"You know, I could always just teleport away," I eventually managed to pant once she'd let me and my breasts go.

"And I would just have to hunt you down like I did last time, before showing you what a *real* punishment is all about," my mate countered without missing a beat, her sharp teeth flashing in amusement. "But you're not going to make me do that, are you, Melody?"

"I..."

The two of us fell into an impromptu staring contest then. One that I lost spectacularly after only a few seconds of direct scrutiny from those fiery, amber-gold eyes.

"No," I murmured as a burst of heat rushed into my face and an excited shiver raced down my spine.

"That's 'No, ma'am' when I'm dealing with you like this," Morgan corrected sternly, accompanying her reprimand with a light but still devastatingly effective flick of her wrist against the pouting lips between my legs.

SLAP!

"Holycrapshootfrick!"

Sending me leaping a full foot into the air.

"Well?" she demanded after I'd calmed down enough from that sudden spike of humiliating stinging to be able to speak in something other than garbled Mormon swears. "Have I made myself clear yet, *pet*, or am I going to have to switch your pussy until you've learned some manners?"

"Yes, ma'am! I mean, no, ma'am! I mean, I'm sorry, ma'am!" I exclaimed in a garbled mess while dancing from foot to foot, my plaintive looks for support from our gathered audience being met with feral grins that unhelpfully resonated as pleasant tingles across my still smarting labia.

"Good girl."

Morgan put a stop to my squirming by wrapping a strong hand around the back of my neck and pulling me in for another short, hungry kiss before easing back a step and holding out her hand.

"Here you go," chirped Sasha, apparently having materialized by her side while I hadn't been paying attention and handing off three switches she'd cut and stripped of leaves.

"Very good." Morgan gave each supple length of thin green branch a few test flicks, all the while keeping her vicious, predatory stare locked straight on me. "Oh yes, very good indeed."

I, on the other hand, jumped in place, my pussy clenching and toes curling with each menacing *SWISH-SWISH! SWISH-SWISH!* The switches made as they cut through the cool night air.

"Um, Morgan, I don't think we-"

But, before I could get whatever weak protest I was only half-willing to make out of my mouth, my mate had me by the hair again and was yanking me around and to the side so that she could start whipping my bare bottom and thighs.

THWIP! THWIP! THWIP!

"Ack! Oh! Crap, shoot, FRICK!"

Oh my gosh! How was something that thin and wimpy so much worse than her hand?!

THWIP! THWIP! THWIP!

"Morgan, please!" I begged, all other thoughts scoured from my mind by that deceptively lightweight lash as I jogged in an increasingly frantic circle around the deck, my breasts bouncing with each hopping step I took.

THWIP! THWIP! THWIP!

"Frick, shoot, owie, owie, owie!"

Despite my dancing and extremely articulate protests, though, I was unable to actually flee from the razor-thin cuts of that evil, evil switch as it assaulted my wobbling backside thanks to my mate's iron-tight hold on my hair. Worse still, I couldn't even reach back to rub at my burning bottom, because my freaking hands were tied together in front of me.

THWIP! THWIP! THWIP!

Which, don't get me wrong, was super-duper-ultra-spicy red hot, and the sensation of that leather belt creaking as it refused to give way while my bottom lit up like a gosh darn pyrotechnics show on the fourth of July was going to live rent free inside my head for the rest of eternity, but it also still freaking *hurt*, dang it!

"I'm sorry, I'm sorry, I'm sorry!"

THWIP! THWIP! THWIP!

"Oh, I'm sure you are," Morgan agreed, picking up the pace so that she was now layering at least three searing lines of fury across the lower half of my bottom and the backs of my thighs every other second as little bits and pieces of broken twig rained down onto the deck.

THWIP! THWIP! THWIP!

"But that doesn't change the fact that this *needs* to happen. Does it, Melody?"

THWIP! THWIP! THWIP!

"DOES IT?" she barked, loud enough that I worried her neighbors might hear and come to see what was going on.

THWIP! THWIP! THWIP!

That visual alone was more than enough to get me howling my reply as fast as I could.

"Yes, ma'am! I'm sorry, ma'am! I'll be good, I'll be good, I'll be gooood!"

THWIP! THWIP! THWIP!

"I know you will, baby."

Morgan's voice was bright and cheery as she tossed aside her first broken switch and replaced it with a fresh one. Resuming her relentless pace, just barely managing to keep ahead of my vampiric healing, she once again set about painting a nonstop, crisscrossing patchwork of long, thin welts against my skin. Welts that flashed sunshine-bright for a split second with their impact (especially when they wrapped around to bite into the significantly less padded side of my hip), before rapidly cooling off into an itchy sort of nothing.

THWIP! THWIP! THWIP!

"Ah, ah, oh! Come onnnn!"

THWIP! THWIP! THWIP!

"Hmmm… Nope. Don't think I will."

THWIP! THWIP! THWIP!

"Agh, you- Ah! *Suck*!"

THWIP! THWIP! THWIP!

"That's really more your thing, but behave yourself and I just might show you where I like to use my lips, batty buns."

THWIP! THWIP! THWIP!

Morgan wasn't actually hurting me (I doubt she could, even if she wanted to), but that dang switch still stung like a french toast mother-father every time it found its mark, making the hand spanking she'd given me the other night seem like nothing by comparison. We had long since blown past my pain tolerance threshold and into the wild blue yonder where my perception of the world around me shrank in to encompass nothing but my furiously burning backside and the sensation of Morgan's hard muscles shifting beneath her skin, propelled along by the ever-present siren song of her blood pumping through her veins as she continued to dish out my punishment with an enthusiasm that was downright flattering (if extremely painful).

THWIP! THWIP! THWIP!

"OMG! You can spank her as hard as you want and it just clears away," gasped Sasha, clapping in delight while bouncing atop Tatiana's lap. "She's like a jiggly Etch a Sketch!"

"She sure is," grunted Morgan, starting to sound slightly out of breath as we rounded the corner into what must have been minute three or four of our dance of dominance and submission. "Which, as you can see-"

THWIP! THWIP! THWIP!

"Makes disciplining her-"

THWIP! THWIP! THWIP!

"Kind of-"

THWIP! THWIP! THWIP!

"Difficult."

"Oooh, I think I might be able to help with that," offered Dani, arching her back as Dorian pawed at her chest through her t-shirt. "Conspiracy nutjobs sell this colloidal silver lotion stuff on the internet. It has microscopic silver particles suspended inside of it that they think can cure cancer or whatever. I bet that'd put a nice dent in her healing factor if you rubbed some into her buns before you got to work."

"What?!" I demanded, my stomach and feet leaping with the suggestion while my face flushed even brighter at the visual she summoned.

THWIP! THWIP! THWIP!

"Hah! That sounds like a fantastic idea."

Apparently growing tired of my ineffective attempts to run away, Morgan tightened her hold on my hair and shoved me over the table where all this trouble had started.

THWIP! THWIP! THWIP!

"Oh my gosh, oh my gosh, oh my gosh!"

Taking advantage of my new position to *really* start giving it to me.

THWIP! THWIP! THWIP!

"Order some for me later tonight, yeah?"

"No, you- Ack! Can't-!" I started to whine.

"Don't be silly, pet. Of course she can."

Morgan then proceeded to shatter the remnants of her second switch against the backs of my thighs.

THWIP! THWIP! THWIP!

"Freaking, owie, shoot, crap!"

THWIP! THWIP! THWIP!

You know, For something that seemed to lose a bit of itself every time it took a bite out of me, those dang twigs lasted a *lot* longer than I would have expected.

"Dani, I want some of that lotion stuff delivered by Friday. Understood?"

Eventually tossing her spent switch aside, Morgan picked up her third and (hopefully) final one, giving it a few test flicks through the air. While, Dani, dutiful as ever, nodded once to her Alpha.

"You got it, girl." Before flashing me an impish grin. "I'll also throw in some capsaicin lotion while I'm at it so you two can really turn up the heat."

"Heh. Great," nodded Morgan, bearing down on the small of my back with her free hand as she cranked up the pace yet again. "Now then-"

THWIP-THWIP-THWIP!

"Let's wrap this up, shall we?"

CHAPTER 9

Morgan

Unsurprisingly, my switch broke down long before Melody ever did. That being said, by the time I tossed the ragged remnants of it aside, breathing hard from the effort of trying to whip at least a modicum of respect for pack hierarchy into her bratty backside, I was pleased to see that I'd managed to at least wring out a couple tears from those beautiful baby blues of hers.

Speaking of moisture...

The hypnotic aroma of her arousal hung thick in the crisp night air around us, sweet and intoxicating, and yet another one of her reflexive vampiric traits working double-time to lure in unsuspecting prey.

Heh. Nice try, pet.

Unintentional or not, I still wasn't about to let my submissive take back control like that. Not after I'd just busted my ass busting *her* ass. So, snatching up those luscious crimson locks while their owner was busy pretending she totally wasn't grinding against the edge of the table in a not so subtle attempt to get herself off, I yanked Melody back to her feet and pushed a hand between her thighs.

"Well, well, well, look who's all hot and bothered after getting her ass switched in front of the pack," I sneered, dragging my fingertips up and down across her sopping folds in a taunting caress that deliberately avoided her clit.

"P-Please, ma'am…"

Melody's breath was coming in short, staccato gasps now as her hips rolled beneath my feather-light touch in search of the friction she needed to push herself over the edge.

"Awww, what's the matter? Does somebody want to come on her Alpha's fingers?"

"Y… Yes!"

"Well, too bad." Drawing back my hand after just barely grazing her hood, I flashed my mate a wicked grin. "I don't think I'm ready to let you come quite yet."

"But...! That's not-!" she started to protest. "Umph!"

That is, until I shoved my glistening fingers inside her shocked O of a mouth.

"Clean up your mess, brat," I ordered, delighted by the way she immediately moved to do as she was told even as her brows dipped together into an adorable glower. "And you'd better keep those fangs to yourself if you don't want me to send Sasha back out for a dozen more switches."

That only half-serious threat was enough to get a truly delectable squeak out of Melody, prompting her to redouble her finger licking efforts. And prompting *me* to redouble my resistance to the urge to shove her back over the table and start taking her immediately.

Soon, I told myself, willing my inner wolf to be patient. *Remember, one step at a time here.*

Much sooner than I would have preferred, we reached the point where Melody was basically just sucking on my fingers for the fun of it rather than because they still had her cum on them, and I reluctantly withdrew them from between those perfectly pouty lips.

"Ready to get these off?" I asked, reaching for where I had her hands bound together in front of her.

To my surprise, she shook her head and took a hesitant couple of steps back. Lifting her hands above her in an attempt to put them out of reach that mostly just succeeded in showing off her breasts.

"Um, do you mind if we don't just yet?"

"Well, if you *insist*," I said with a shrug, not at all trying to hide my amusement as I watched her erect nipples sway from side to side. "Any particular reason why, though? Not that they don't look great on you, babe, but if I leave you like this for much longer, I don't think I'm going to be able to stop myself from mounting you right here on the deck."

Melody's face erupted into a vibrant shade of red that reached the tips of her ears as I made a show of raking my gaze down her naked body. Devouring the mouth-watering sights of her heavy breasts and clean-shaven pussy as I licked my lips, before locking eyes with her once again.

"You think you're ready for that?" I pressed, growing suddenly serious. "I promise I won't be upset if you want to wait. Like I said, I'm happy to go at whatever pace makes you feel comfortable."

"I, um..."

Despite her apparent newfound love of bondage, I still fully expected Melody to say no, assuming it would take at least a few more dates before we went all the way. But, much to my pleasant surprise, she instead squared her shoulders and narrowed her eyes at me with a spark of (rather ironic, given the circumstances) defiance.

"Bring it."

Holy shit, how did I ever get this lucky?

"Bring it, huh?"

Grinning with evil purpose now, I padded leisurely after my mate's retreating form like the predator cornering its prey that I was, maneuvering her around to the chair we'd been sharing earlier and pushing her into it. She went down easily enough, and I only felt a mild twinge of annoyance when she didn't wince as her unmarked cheeks made rough contact with the chair's criss-crossing wrought iron seat.

"So, you're telling me you *want* to be bound and helpless while I do whatever I want to you?" I crooned, caging her in on either side with my hands on the arms of the chair. We both knew the answer to that question, but I still wanted to hear her say it out loud. "Well?"

In response, Melody's pupils dilated to the size of dinner plates and her irises turned an eerie, iridescent crimson.

"Oh? Did I touch a nerve?"

My grin grew wider then, while my instincts screamed at me that I was tempting fate by so flagrantly taunting the hungry animal lurking behind that shy smile. I didn't care, though. My inner wolf was more than ready to pin her down and make her submit if that was how she wanted to play this.

"Could it be that my sweet Melody wants to be unable to run away while I slowly, oh so *slowly*, run my tongue all up and down her defenseless pussy, twirling it around her clit just firmly enough to make her tremble, before I start pushing my fingers inside of her one… by… one?"

"Oh gosh, um, I, um-"

"Or maybe you'd like me to bend you over and spread those big, round cheeks as wide as they'll go so the girls and I can all get a good long look at that tight, virgin asshole of yours before I fuck it so hard you'll be walking with a limp for the rest of the week?"

"I- That's not-!"

Her entire body spasmed with that one, and I made a mental note to circle back to it sometime later.

"Of course..." Moving in for the kill, I pressed a knee between her thighs, bending her back into a breathless arch as I ground against her damp core. "Maybe what you *really* want is to not have any choice at all? Hmm? Maybe deep down you're just a dirty church girl *slut* who wants me to use her over and over and *over* again until all she can think about is how good it feels when I'm coming inside of her?"

"I, I, I-!"

Our gazes snapped together in a silent battle of wills for I don't even know how long then, her trying not to come while her hips shifted against my thigh of their own accord and me just daring her to deny what I'd said, before she eventually cracked and a wave of icy blue washed away the vampiric red.

"Yes please," she whimpered, collapsing back into her chair and breathing heavily.

"What was that?" Cupping a hand to my ear, I sent a wink in the direction of my rapt pack mates before leaning in closer. "Speak up now. The girls and I all want to hear you say it nice and loud."

Melody gave a small start at that, apparently having forgotten all about our audience. But, to her credit, she pushed through her embarrassment enough to answer in a voice that only shook a little, "I… I want you to use me however you want."

Fucking. Score.

"Are you sure?"

I kept my voice low and husky as I slipped a hand inside my shorts and began to grind the heel of my palm against my own thoroughly-soaked pussy, maintaining eye contact with my trembling mate the entire time as I did so.

"It's going to be a lot rougher on you if we do it this way," I warned, a breathy hitch creeping its way into my words as I found my groove. God, the way she was staring up at me with those perpetual dark bags beneath her luminous eyes was so fucking hot. "I won't be using my fingers this time."

At Melody's confused look, I remembered that she hadn't been raised by wolves like I had, and decided that it would probably easier to just show her what I had planned instead of trying to put it into words. So, I pushed my shorts and underwear halfway down my thighs.

"Wh-Wh-What the heck is *that*?!"

Melody's eyes once again went wide as could be as ten elongated inches of rapidly-engorging werewolf breeding clit bobbed free to hover only a scant few inches away from her partially-parted lips.

"It's just my clit," I reassured her while my pack burst into uproarious laughter, drinking in every maidenly blush and curious grimace that crossed her delicate features as she sat there staring in fascination while I stroked my hand up and down my arousal-slicked length. "Didn't they teach sex ed back in Mormon school?"

"Not like that-!" she started to protest, earning those lips pouting up at me from between her lewdly parted thighs another sharp *SLAP!* That had her cutting loose with the most delicious yelp.

It was so tasty, in fact, that I couldn't help going in for seconds.

SLAP!

"Ah!"

And, what the hell? Why not thirds?

SLAP!

"Frick-shoot-dang-crap!" Melody hissed before I took her mouth in another rough kiss that had her moaning for more by the time I let her go.

All of this did absolutely nothing to diminish just how hard I was for her, and I knew I was going to go straight up vampire-mauling feral any second now if I didn't do something about it. Still, I had enough presence of mind to remember that I needed to make sure Melody and I were both on the same page before we went any further. This wasn't some casual rut between pack mates, after all. This was my mate's first time.

This was *Melody's* first time.

"Focus, hon," I admonished with an unrepentant half-grin, kneading those perfect handfuls of breasts in my palms. "As you can see, werewolf anatomy is a bit different than what you're probably used to. At least, Dominant werewolf anatomy is. I know it's probably a bit of a shock, but this is still just my clit. If it helps, just think of it as a strap-on I can summon up at will, yeah?"

"O-Okay..." Melody managed, starting to relax. "That seems like it could... Like it could be-"

She moaned long and low as I twirled my thumbs over her nipples.

"Useful."

"And how," I agreed with a genuine laugh despite my best efforts to keep the whole smoldering Alpha sex beast thing going. "*Technically*, it's intended for popping pups into the wombs of submissive and breedable wolves like Sasha over there."

I hooked a thumb over my shoulder with that remark, indicating the bubbly blonde who was far too busy having her shorts and panties shredded by an impatient Tatiana while Dorian shoved her own clit between those smart-ass lips of hers to really complain properly.

"But, they work great for stress relief too."

"Oh my gosh are they really going to-?"

Apparently, I wasn't the only one who'd noticed what was going on among the three of them (not that they were exactly being subtle), because Melody's mouth was now hanging open as she watched Tatiana push into Sasha her from behind with the sort of hard shove that had the poor, slutty Omega gagging on Dorian's clit.

"Oh! Um, never mind, I guess they are."

Mmph, now *that* was a tasty visual. Maybe Dani and I could recreate it with Melody later?

"Hey, focus," I laughed, ignoring my own hypocrisy as I snapped my fingers in front of my drooling mate.

"Oops, sorry!" she started to apologize, still only half paying attention as her gaze started to flicker crimson again. "Uh, what were you, um... saying...?"

Uh-oh. That's a literal red flag if ever I've seen one.

Truth be told, it was probably a miracle Melody hadn't gone all fangs out on any of us yet with how badly I'd been winding her up. Fortunately, I was pretty sure I knew exactly how to keep her mind (and appetite) occupied.

"Right, then."

Sweeping my sweaty fringe out of my eyes with a savage grin, I bent down and gathered up my thoroughly distracted mate's legs. Hoisting her ankles and knees up past her shoulders, and raising her hips clear off the seat of the deck chair I'd cornered her in.

"Ready?" I asked, drinking in the mingled look of shock, fear, and excitement that flashed across her pale face as we locked eyes once again.

I definitely had her full attention now.

"Wait, Morgan! I, um, I, um-!"

"Yes or no?"

Submissive as Melody might be, I still wasn't about to take her without her explicitly saying that she was okay with it, even if she *was* dribbling cum onto the chair beneath her. That didn't mean I couldn't rub my clit between the damp folds of her slit, though.

"Ah! Fu-rick! I-!"

Which, in retrospect, might have been a mistake given how it seemed to short-circuit her brain, making her eyes flash in the dark before she managed to gasp.

"Yes!"

"Say it," I growled, digging my nails into the backs of her chubby thighs. "Tell me what you want."

"Oh gosh, please... please fuck me!" Melody squeaked, and oh my god if that wasn't the most adorable thing I'd ever heard.

I'd even managed to get her to swear too!

"You got it." I felt her suck in a shallow breath then as I began to line up the tip of my throbbing clit with the base of her opening. "Hang on tight now, pet. We've got more than a week's worth of me wanting to fuck your brains out to get through before we're done here."

That managed to draw out a yelp of mingled panic and lust

from Melody, and I used her momentary distraction to push all the way up to the hilt inside of her in one hard thrust that had her screaming my name into my mouth as I captured her lips in the sort of all-consuming kiss that had the rest of the world falling away.

Oh yeah, she'd definitely been worth the wait.

And, oh my fuck, was she ever *tight*.

Jesus, she really was a virgin, wasn't she? Though, thankfully, one who'd apparently lost her hymen at some point long before now. So, you know, a naughty virgin.

That definitely fit.

Speaking of fitting…

Gritting my teeth to stave off coming immediately (she wasn't the only one who was close!) I started to ease my hips back while I held her in place by my grip on her ass. Carefully, I withdrew nearly the entire length of my not insubstantial clit from her eager if inexperienced slit, before shoving it all the way back into her in one smooth thrust that bucked her roughly against the wrought iron deck chair.

"M-Morgan-! Oh gosh, oh crap!"

"Shhh, I've got you, baby."

"I-! I-! Ah!" she cried as I started slamming into her rippling cheeks at a steady interval. "Oh gosh, p-please, don't stop."

"Wasn't… planning on it."

Her arms were yanking so hard at her restraints, but my belt and silver necklace were refusing to budge, and in her desperation as her mind was overrun by pure, unfiltered pleasure (shut up, I know I'm a good lay) her head lolled back to expose her lily white throat. And, holy shit, was the urge to bite down and spill my seed inside of her hard to resist. She would absolutely love it, I was sure, especially if her initial reaction to the mate bite I'd given her after our first "date" was anything to go by, but I also knew I couldn't risk it. Even if the chances of me impregnating her were extremely low (werewolf fertility is notoriously fickle, and from what I'd read since talking to Mom, werewolf and vampires attempting to couple is even worse), the chance still wasn't zero, and I wasn't about to risk something like that without Melody and I having a serious conversation about it first.

Not that I was even close to ready for kids, but still. Communication is important.

"Are you close?" I grunted instead, mesmerized by the way her breasts rolled and bounced with each rhythmic pump in and out of her absolutely perfect pussy.

We'd only been going at it for a couple minutes, but I'd like to think I'd gotten pretty good at reading her body language by that point, and I was pretty sure she was going to blow any second now.

"Yes! Oh my gosh, YES!"

See? What'd I tell you?

"Come for me then," I growled into her shoulder, breathing in the mingled pheromones of our mate bite while she howled at the top of her lungs and her inner walls clamped down around me, squeezing my clit for dear life as she came like a tidal wave, dragging me down with her.

"Fuck, Melody, I'm-!"

I tried my best to hold off for as long as I could, wanting to give her the chance to bask in the sensation of being as full and complete as she made me feel every time we were together for as long as possible. However, it soon dawned on me that it was either now or never, and I just managed to pull out of her with a knee-buckling gasp in time to spill my cum all over her face.

"Oh god... Oh fuck...!"

That. Was. Incredible.

Unfortunately, I only had one brief, beautiful moment to take in the decadent glory of that visual, my seed dribbling down Melody's chin and onto her heaving tits in the most lewd display of submission I'd ever seen, before her eyes flashed a practically neon crimson and she launched herself at me with a snarl.

Even with her wrists still bound together, Melody was absurdly strong, and she had zero problems taking us both down to the ground. Where she then proceeded to sink her fangs deep into my jugular.

"Shit-fuck!"

It was… Honestly, it was a really weird sensation to feel my blood literally being sucked out of my neck like the world's most attractive sippy cup, but the roiling cascade of back-to-back orgasms that accompanied the involuntary blood donation more than made up for any mild discomfort.

Coming so close on the heels of my last orgasm, you'd think I'd have been able to handle myself just a little bit better. But, nope, Melody absolutely floored my ass, leaving me a twitching, drooling mess while she drank her fill, the little brat. That being said, though, I wasn't *totally* out of control this time. For starters, not being hypnotized helped a lot, and after what I assumed had to be about a minute (or maybe a day? Time was starting to get a bit fuzzy around the edges the longer things went on), I knew I needed to bring my thirsty mate back under control before it was too late. While I could trust her to feed from any of the other girls without completely losing herself to the experience, Mom had explained to me that Pack Alpha blood was in a league all its own.

Which was both flattering, and also very bad if I didn't want to end the night hemorrhaging all over the deck.

"Sorry, babe." Unsheathing my claws, I sank them into the soft and bouncy bottom straddling my stomach. While Melody, in turn, squealed into my neck. Which, I'll tell you for free, *also* felt really fucking weird. Especially when she did a spit take with my own blood. "Had to… to pull you back."

"Th-Thanks," she gasped after unlatching from me, any unwanted assault on her ass already forgotten about as she licked my puncture wounds closed and collapsed on top of me in a boneless heap. "I'm just going to… to… rest my eyes for a…"

And, just like that, my deflowered Draculina was out like a light.

"Sleep tight," I murmured into her hair, enveloping her smaller frame in a fierce, loving hug before rolling us over to get a better view of the ongoing fuck-fest that the rest of my pack had devolved into while I'd been otherwise occupied.

Apparently, Dani had decided to get in on the fun as well. She'd slipped in behind Tatiana, and was now pounding her in the ass with the sort of ruthless enthusiasm that made her my Second. Truth be told, it was pretty impressive that all four of them had managed to find a rhythm that worked for them, considering that while Tatiana was in the process of getting fucked, she and Dorian were also making out over where they were still spit-roasting Sasha.

God, I love a good barbecue…

CHAPTER 10

Melody

Much like the last time I'd gotten totally drunk off my butt on Morgan's sweet, sweet O negative, I woke up an indeterminate number of hours later in her bed, jelly-limbed and utterly content. Whatever Alpha werewolf goodness she had flowing through her veins sure packed one heck of a punch, but that was just fine with me. After all, I liked it when she hit me.

Well, okay, not like *hit* me, hit me, but- Look. You know what I mean. I liked it when she spanked me and called me pet and stuff, all right?

Good?

Good.

Anyway, I'd apparently been out of it for a lot longer than I thought I had, because I was starting to get that itchy feeling at the back of my head that meant the sun was on its way up the eastern horizon. Normally, that would have sent me scrambling for home as soon as possible lest I wind up with a blistering sunburn and a skull-shattering migraine. But, in that moment, I really wasn't in much of a mood to do anything.

In fact, I was right where I wanted to be.

Morgan's bed was so much more comfortable than mine was, *and* she'd installed a truly wonderful set of blackout curtains since the last time I'd been over. They plunged her spacious bedroom into near total darkness, with only the dim light from a single desk lamp to keep the shadows at bay while I lay there curled up beneath the covers.

Mmmm... A girl could get used to this.

Rolling over, I let out a long yawn and arched my back in a full-body stretch, only belatedly realizing that I was still naked when my nipples grazed the soft material of her comforter. Again, though, that was just fine with me. I was way too drained to really give a crap about something as trivial as modesty. And, really, after everything that had gone down tonight, I was starting to realize I rather liked being on display. Besides, there were much more interesting things to focus on just then other than how I was breaking the Law of Chastity in about six or seven different ways.

Like, Morgan, for instance.

She was sitting at her desk, the sharply-defined slopes of her broad shoulders subtly rippling and shifting beneath the smooth olive skin exposed by her racerback tank top as she typed away on her laptop. My vision was still a little blurry from my blood bender, but it looked to me like she was making edits to a dissertation exploring the finer points of post-modern impressionism and how it related to South American indigenous folk art.

Ah, right, Art History PhD. That makes sense...

Not wanting to interrupt, I kept quiet and watched her work for what felt like an extremely cozy eternity. Luxuriating in the way her lips would occasionally purse into a concentrating frown as she read and reread a sentence, making minor adjustments to word choice and placement, or else how she'd sometimes bear her teeth in a snarl whenever she came to a note from her advisor that she didn't like.

"Hey there, babe. You back in the land of the living?" she eventually asked, reaching a stopping point on her paper and saving it before closing her laptop.

"For the moment," I yawned in return with another stretch. "It's getting kinda late."

"Tell me about it."

My heart leapt inside my chest as Morgan swiveled around in her seat to face me, a gentle smile softening her usually sharp features into something that felt safe and comfortable.

I must've been staring, because the next thing I knew, her smile had turned teasing.

"See something you like?"

"Maaaaybe."

Speaking of wanting, all *I* wanted just then was to be close to her. So, before I could second guess myself, I threw back the covers and rolled out of bed and onto the floor.

"Want some company?"

Gazing up at Morgan through messed up bangs, I watched as a wave of lust darkened those amber-gold eyes I'd fallen in love with. A lust that reverberated deep inside of me, sending a frisson of arousal directly between my thighs as her smile widened into something delightfully sinister.

Why, Grandma, what big teeth you have...

"Come here," she ordered, crooking a finger.

"R... Right!"

The next thing I knew, I was crawling toward her on all fours, my chest and hips swaying with my every movement as I closed the distance between us until I was kneeling between her parted legs with my hands folded demurely in my lap and my upper arms pushing my breasts together and out.

"Um, hi."

"Morning, beautiful."

I guess it probably shouldn't have come as a surprise to me that being on my knees like this before my mate felt so natural. She *was* an Alpha, after all.

My Alpha.

"You, um... You aren't mad at me, are you?"

"Huh?" Morgan's brows furrowed in confusion, before just as quickly smoothing out as she barked out a short laugh. "Oh! For feeding on me?"

"Um, yeah."

I licked my lips, all too aware of just how sharp my fangs were inside my mouth right then.

"Of course I'm not. Why would I be?"

"Well, I mean, you'd just gotten through punishing me for not respecting your authority as the pack leader," I explained, unable to meet her eye as I shifted my weight from one bare cheek to the other and back again. "And, um, I kinda, sorta, totally took your blood without permission in front of everyone?"

"Oh, Melody." Sifting her fingers through my sleep-tousled hair, Morgan looked down at me with a soft and reassuring smile. "I would never be mad at you for acting on your instincts."

Sagging against her thigh, I let out an exhausted but happy sigh.

"Really?"

Honestly, part of me was a little disappointed that she wasn't going to spank me again. While the rest of me was way too busy being relieved that she wasn't angry. I really hadn't meant to go after her like that, after all. It had just sort of… happened.

"Look. We aren't human. I never was, and you aren't anymore," Morgan said, her tone growing serious as she continued to stroke my hair. "We are what we are, and *you*, my dear, are-"

"A slutty church girl who gets off by feeding on the blood of the innocent?"

"I was going to say 'just fine the way you are,' but that works too."

"Oh."

Great. I'd been trying to lighten the mood, and now I just felt like crap for putting myself down.

Ugh! Why is that always my go-to move?

"Besides, calling me or Tatiana 'innocent' definitely seems like a bit of a stretch, wouldn't you agree?" added Morgan, nipping my burgeoning spike of self-loathing in the bud with a wink. "Also, just for the record, I *love* that you're a slutty church girl who gets off by feeding on the blood of the innocent, sinful, and just plain attractive. Those fangs look so fucking hot on you, and the nonstop orgasms that come with them are a nice bonus."

Okay, I laughed at that. I couldn't help it. "Whatever you say, 'Alpha'," I started to fire back, my sass cranking back up to eleven complete with air quotes, before screeching to a halt as I was jerked a full inch off the carpet by my hair. "Ack!"

"Am I going to have to remind you where your place in the pack hierarchy is, again, *pet*?"

Morgan's tone had taken on the sort of dangerous singsong to it that would have no doubt soaked my panties through if I'd been wearing any at the time. And, again, part of me was unbelievably tempted to call her bluff as she leaned in to none too gently clamp her jaws around my throat. But, the rest of me (my submissive side, I guess?) was already speeding ahead with yelping out, "No, ma'am! Sorry, ma'am!"

"Heh. That's what I thought."

Smirking in evident self-satisfaction, my mate kissed me just long enough to trace her tongue across my teeth, teasing at the tip of one fang, before letting me go and resuming her hair stroking.

We stayed like that for what felt like a very long time after that. Neither of us really feeling the need to say much of anything as we let ourselves be swept away by the low hum of the house's central heating pushing back the night's chill. Tranquil and unhurried, and also maybe still a little horny from that unexpected show of dominance, I sat there with my face nestled against the inside of one of Morgan's flannel-covered thighs. Letting myself be lulled into a dose by the steady, reassuring *thump-thump, thump-thump, thump-thump* of my mate's pulse while she continued to play with my hair; occasionally dragging her nails across my scalp and making me shiver.

"Soooo, can we talk?"

Blinking blearily up at Morgan, I fought to shake off the heavy shroud of fatigue that had settled over me. Much as I wanted to give in to day drain and crawl back into bed, we still had things we needed to figure out. And, for better or worse, there was no time like the present.

"Of course we can." Morgan proceeded to ruin the order she'd made of my bedhead by giving it a frond ruffle. "What's on your mind? The mate bite thing?"

"The mate bite thing, yeah."

Breathing out a sigh of relief that she'd been the one to say it and not me, I eased in just a bit closer and twined my arms and legs around the steady support of her calf.

"Soooo?"

"Yessss?"

Morgan's mouth quirked to the side in a cocky half grin that warmed me thoroughly from the inside out. It was also clear that she wasn't about to do anything more than that. Apparently, if I wanted to talk, I was actually going to have to, you know, talk.

Rude.

"Well..."

Without realizing I'd started doing it, I fingered the series of tooth-sized bruises that formed a twin pair of crescent moons around where my right shoulder met my neck. Touching them seemed to grant me an extra measure of calm, and whether that was just in my head or not didn't really matter to me. This was serious stuff we were dealing with here, and I needed all the help I could get.

"Does this mean that we're, like, married?" I finally asked, deciding to start with what seemed like the biggest hurdle first and work my way down from there.

"Hmmm…" Morgan made a see-sawing gesture with her hand. "Sort of."

"Sort of?"

"Well, in werewolf society, a mate bite marks a pack member's, well, mate. Which, I suppose, is more or less the equivalent of a human spouse? Like, a mate is a partner for life. Someone you rely on more than anybody else, and who you may or may not, you know, *mate* with."

She shrugged.

"As for the bite itself, I guess human wedding bands are a good comparison, yeah. Though, in this case, it's not just an aesthetic symbol. Our mate bite combines our personal pheromones together into a unique chemical signature that lets every other wolf know that you've been claimed."

"Is that, um..." My stomach fluttered with that last word. I liked the way it sounded, even if it raised the temperature in my face by about a million degrees. "Is that important?"

"Depending on the pack and the wolf, it can be," nodded Morgan. "Wolves don't approach sex the same way most humans do. For us, it's a lot more straightforward and casual. Basically, when a Dominant is aroused, our instinct is to find a submissive and fuck them until we're satisfied."

"Submissives like Sasha?" I asked, more fascinated than hesitant now as I vaguely recalled what Morgan had mentioned during her brief explanation of her and the other's uniquely werewolfish clitorises.

"Yep! Aside from you, she and Tatiana to a lesser degree are the only submissives in the house right now. So, as you can probably imagine, they wind up getting used by the rest of us pretty regularly in between their studies. Hell, sometimes not even in between. I distinctly remember fucking Sasha while she was taking an online quiz once. Which she passed, amusingly enough.

"And, yes, before you ask, she and Tatiana always have the final say on whether or not they rut with us. I can't stand packs that operate on might makes right when it comes to breeding rules. We practice enthusiastic consent around here."

"Oh, um, that's good to know."

The idea that one of Morgan's wolves might force themselves on someone else without their permission hadn't even occurred to me, but it was still reassuring to know that she ran a tight and egalitarian ship. Honestly, rather than getting caught up on consent, I'd been a little too busy fantasizing about my mate pumping in and out of the bubbly blonde while she was bent over a desk.

I suppose that probably should have made me jealous, but I just… wasn't.

Maybe it's a vampire thing? I mused, recalling the half-gagged moans Sasha had been making earlier and blushing even harder. *I mean, it's not like I don't routinely thirst after just about every pretty girl I see, so it would make sense.*

"Um, are Dani and Dorian going to want to, you know…"

"Fuck you?" Morgan finished for me with a knowing smirk.

The warmth in my cheeks deepening to downright dangerous levels, I nodded up at her with a faux-pout.

"Yeah, *that*."

"Only if you want to, pet." Leaning down, Morgan pressed a kiss to my forehead, smoothing out my consternation. "You're easily the most submissive one in the pack right now, and under other circumstances that would make you a walking target for every other Dominant in a twenty mile radius, some submissives too come to think of it. But, since you've been claimed, they'll be able to scent that and will understand that it's not okay to try and coax you into rutting with them."

Her teeth flashed at me then, pointed and sharp and just a little bit feral in the semi-dark.

"Of course, if someone *did* try anything like that without your consent first, I'd rip their fucking throat out."

"R-Really?"

Blanching at that visual, I did my best to swallow the sudden burst of bats Morgan's remark produced within me.

"Really."

"That, um, that wouldn't be good."

"No, probably not," my mate agreed with just a touch of wry amusement. "Situations like that are pretty rare these days, though. At least among the pack I grew up in. Sometimes a Dominant will try to nose their way into a polycule they're not welcome in, and will wind up getting their ass kicked for it, but that's usually about the worst of it. So, try not to stress, yeah? I promise I won't flip my shit if Dani or Dorian ask if they can take a crack at you."

"Phew!" Hearing that really was a relief. The last thing I wanted was to stir up drama between my girlfriend / werewolf wife and my new friends by getting a bit too flirty. "Wait. What's a polycule?"

First pheromones, and now polycules? Geez, there was a lot more chemistry involved in werewolf relationship dynamics than I ever would have expected.

"Like what Dorian and Tatiana have with Sasha."

"Oh! Polycule, as in poly*amory*."

Okay, yeah. That made way more sense.

"Exactly."

"But, wait a minute, wasn't Dani-?" I started to ask, before being cut off by another laugh from Morgan.

"Oh god, for someone so wantonly horny, you sure are an innocent little flower sometimes." Grinning down at me, she glided the pad of her thumb over my cheekbone. "Just because we lay claim to each other with mate bites, that doesn't mean we can't share when we feel like it. Those three are in a committed relationship with each other, sure, but they've also made the decision as a group that they don't mind having Dani, or me for that matter, slipping into the mix whenever one of them is in the mood for it. Which, honestly, can be pretty useful. Tatiana, for instance, loves to take it in the ass, but Dorian isn't really into that and Sasha isn't a Dominant, so Dani, er... fills that gap, so to speak."

"Ah. I, uh... I see."

I was pretty sure my face was hot enough by this point to set Morgan's pajama pants on fire if I wasn't careful. Fortunately, just then I was presented with a perfect change in topic.

"Um, excuse me, what the heck is *that*?" I demanded, my embarrassment all but forgotten about as I jabbed a finger toward the twin, fang-sized bruises visible on the side of Morgan's neck.

"Heh. Finally noticed those, did you?" she asked, looking pleased.

"They're kinda hard to miss," I replied, still confused.

Hard to miss, and theoretically impossible.

Whenever I'd used my blood to seal someone's puncture wounds after feeding from them in the past, they'd completely disappeared after only a couple of seconds. It's the main reason why I've managed to stay under the radar for so long despite having fed off of seemingly half the campus's jogging population over the last six months. But, Morgan's neck hadn't healed.

Well, it had.

Sort of.

Just not all the way.

"It's a mate bite!" I gasped, things suddenly clicking into place.

Look. Cut me some slack. Sunrise was in full swing, and my brain wasn't firing on all cylinders anymore.

"Sure is, batty buns." Morgan's smile as she said that was bright enough to light up the room. "You tagged me fair and square tonight, and now I'm claimed the same as you."

Well, I guess turnabout is fair play and all that jazz.

"Okay, so… We're werewolf married?"

"That's pretty much the long and the short of it, yep." Looking thoroughly pleased with herself, my mate pushed my hair back out of my eyes. "You know, part of me knew from the moment we first met that you and I were meant for each other. My inner wolf had been screaming at me to bend you over that bar and make you mine the moment you started talking, and after you tried proving you could overpower me, I just couldn't resist."

"Your…" I blinked up at her. "Your wolf?"

"Metaphorical wolf," she corrected herself, rolling her eyes. "You know, the amalgamation of instincts, cultural norms, and biochemistry that makes a werewolf a werewolf."

"Ah." As I mulled that over, another thought hit me. "Wait a minute! If your inner wolf or whatever is just a metaphor, does that mean you can't transform?"

"Of course I can transform!" Morgan actually sounded offended as she said that. "It's just a bit hard for a seven foot wall of furry muscle, teeth, and claws to go unnoticed out here in the suburbs is all."

"Heh. Fair point."

Okay, but I definitely wanted to see *that* now.

"So, uh… yeah."

Blowing out a breath, feeling surprisingly comfortable with having been unwittingly roped into a supernatural marriage pact, I let my body relax back into Morgan's as I only halfheartedly tossed out the next worry that bubbled up.

"Isn't this all still really sudden? Like, I know my parents only dated for a month before they got married, but they're Mormons. They're not, you know…"

"Werewolves? Vampires?"

"I was going to say 'normal', but that works too."

Morgan's cocky grin returned with a vengeance.

"As far as wolves go, mate bonds are established pretty fast. It's less of a 'let's go out on a few dates and see if we like each other' thing, and more of a 'we have literal chemistry between the two of us' sort of thing. So, when you've found your mate, you tend to just… know, and there's no point in trying to fight it."

She accompanied that last bit with a suggestive eyebrow waggle that had me tightening my thighs around her calf in an unconscious attempt to hide the wetness visible between them.

"All right, fair," I conceded, pausing to mull everything over before continuing. "But, what if we want to break up later? Is there werewolf divorce court?"

"Mated wolves don't do break ups, but I'm not going to force you to stay with me if that's not what you want." The hurt and worry that crumpled Morgan's usually confident features as she said that nearly broke my heart. "*Is* that what you want?"

"What? No! Of course it isn't!" I replied immediately, my words coming out a lot more forcefully than I'd intended for them to before my flash of indignation snuffed itself out and I looked away, grimacing. "I just don't want you to regret picking me is all."

"Never." The steely glare that accompanied that declaration made my stomach lurch and my heart leap. "Our relationship might not have started out how either of us expected it to, but we're here now, and I love you, Melody Harper. I don't think I could ever stop loving you."

"I… I…" Stuttering, at a total loss for words, my vision clouded with happy tears. "Oh, Morgan, I love you too!"

Dissipating into black mist, I reappeared straddling my mate's lap, grinding my naked core against her washboard abs as I clung to her for all I was worth.

"And I'm yours."

"You're mine," she growled, nuzzling me back before threading her fingers through my hair, pulling my head back so that I was forced to meet her gaze while her other hand dipped down to cup my pussy. "Now and always."

"Now and always," I agreed breathlessly, suddenly eager for her to take me again despite my mounting day drain as I reached up to run my fingers through my mate's chestnut locks. "You know… The sun is up. I'm going to have to go to sleep pretty soon."

"Oh really now?" That was all the prodding Morgan needed. The next thing I knew, I was bouncing face first down onto the bed. Onto *our* bed. "In that case, I suppose I'll just have to think of something to keep you up past your bedtime, won't I?"

Throwing a saucy smirk back over my shoulder, my heart skipped about a million beats all at once as Morgan's pajama bottoms hit the floor and her massive werewolf girlcock (holy crap, when did I get so lewd?!) began to engorge, glistening with arousal and ready to be put to work. Half a heartbeat after that, her tank top joined her pajamas bottoms, and I just about went into full on cardiac arrest as I finally got my first proper look at the most beautiful pair of breasts I'd ever seen.

"I don't know, I'm pretty tired..." I triedv to taunt, my voice catching as my mouth began to water. "If all you've got is that little thing, I might just, you know... pass out."

"Is that right?"

Arching a brow, Morgan ran her hand up and down her erect length in a way that had my own clit twitching with sudden need.

"Mmhmm." I nodded, only half feigning a yawn. "Hear that? I'm slipping away. Oh noooo."

"You know, I was *going* to take it easy on you and be gentle this time. But, clearly, that's not what you need. Is it, pet?"

"Oh? Was last time not gentle?"

Morgan's eyes flashed bright gold with that, her teeth once again sharpening into deadly points that I knew would fit perfectly against the impressions on my shoulder.

"All right, yep, that's it," she laughed, taking my bait hook, line, and sinker all the while as she matched me feral, predatory grin for feral, predatory grin. "This is going right up your ass, you little brat."

"Hah!"

Score.

I wiggled my butt.

"I'm not afraid of the big bad wolf. Fuh-reaking bring it."

"Just try and stop me."

Roughly grabbing a cheek in either hand, Morgan squeezed hard enough to make me gasp, before pulling said cheeks apart to expose my tightly puckered bottom hole to her ravenous gaze.

"Eep!"

She paused then, her hungry snarl softening into pure, heartfelt adoration.

"I love you, Melody."

"I love you too, Morgan," I sighed. "Now and always."

"Now and always."

Then, keeping me exposed the entire time as she did so (because why wouldn't she?), my mate leaned forward and captured my lips in one last lingering kiss. One that was soft and gentle, and everything I'd ever wanted.

In that moment, I was safe.

In that moment, I was happy.

In that moment, I was *hers*.

"Welcome home."

THE END

www.ingramcontent.com/pod-product-compliance
Lightning Source LLC
Chambersburg PA
CBHW060559310726
48982CB00008B/1171/J

* 9 7 8 1 7 3 3 9 3 5 0 9 8 *